# The Path to the Duke's Heart

## A Clean Regency Romance Novel

*Jonathan Grantham*
*Genevieve Ellsworth*

## Martha Barwood

Copyright © 2024 by Martha Barwood
All Rights Reserved.
This book may not be reproduced or transmitted in any form without the written permission of the publisher. In no way is it legal to reproduce, duplicate, or transmit any part of this document in either electronic means or in printed format. Recording of this publication is strictly prohibited and any storage of this document is not allowed unless with written permission from the publisher.

# Table of Contents

PROLOGUE ............................................................................................ 4
CHAPTER 1 .......................................................................................... 10
CHAPTER 2 .......................................................................................... 17
CHAPTER 3 .......................................................................................... 24
CHAPTER 4 .......................................................................................... 30
CHAPTER 5 .......................................................................................... 36
CHAPTER 6 .......................................................................................... 42
CHAPTER 7 .......................................................................................... 48
CHAPTER 8 .......................................................................................... 55
CHAPTER 9 .......................................................................................... 61
CHAPTER 10 ........................................................................................ 67
CHAPTER 11 ........................................................................................ 73
CHAPTER 12 ........................................................................................ 79
CHAPTER 13 ........................................................................................ 86
CHAPTER 14 ........................................................................................ 92
CHAPTER 15 ........................................................................................ 98
CHAPTER 16 ...................................................................................... 104
CHAPTER 17 ...................................................................................... 110
CHAPTER 18 ...................................................................................... 116
CHAPTER 19 ...................................................................................... 122
CHAPTER 20 ...................................................................................... 128
CHAPTER 21 ...................................................................................... 134
CHAPTER 22 ...................................................................................... 143
CHAPTER 23 ...................................................................................... 150

| | |
|---|---|
| CHAPTER 24 | 155 |
| CHAPTER 25 | 163 |
| EPILOGUE | 168 |
| EXTENDED EPILOGUE | 175 |

# PROLOGUE

*Six years ago...*

Genevieve's laughter, as light and melodious as the spring breeze, intertwined with Harry's youthful giggles. Their playful banter echoed near the stables of Graftonshire, a world of innocence and wonder where everything felt right, light, and blissful. The sun, radiant and benevolent, bathed the sprawling North Eastern estate in golden warmth, making both the children happy and extremely carefree.

At fourteen years of age, Genevieve felt the weight of responsibility for her younger brother, Harry. It rested heavily on her shoulders. It had been four years since their mother had succumbed to tuberculosis, leaving a void that could never truly be filled. Her love for Harry was unwavering, and she would do anything to protect him and ensure his happiness, despite this magnificent loss in their lives.

She watched with awe, knowing her mother would be happy to see them both right now, enjoying their time together. Harry, with his eyes filled with wonder, was chasing a butterfly with all the enthusiasm of a child who saw magic in the simplest of things. His giggles filled the air, a melody of happiness, making Genevieve smile too.

"Do not trip over," she called out as she watched Harry race off. He could be a little clumsy, often tripping over his feet. But Genevieve did not wish to hold him back. She wanted Harry to flourish and learn what he could and could not do. If she did not teach him that lesson, she was not sure who would. Their father was a seasoned diplomat and a revered figure in the British court. He loved his children greatly, they both knew that, but his work kept him away from home a lot of the time.

Genevieve inhaled deeply, breathing in the fragrant blooms. The gardeners made sure that there was always a vibrant scene outside of their manor, and Genevieve loved that. She glanced around the land, allowing a particularly beautiful flower to distract her, pulling her away from her brother for just a brief moment.

She knelt down beside the flower, her fingers delicately brushing its soft petals. It was a moment of reflection, a memory that her mother's stories often stirred within her. The tale her mother used to read to her was one of a handsome prince who showed his love for a princess by giving her a flower very much like this one. It was a simple gesture, but it held great significance. The story had always filled her young heart with dreams of love, adventure, and the possibility of a prince of her own.

As she gazed at the flower, a wistful smile graced her lips. The expectations of her prominent family and their societal status were never far from her mind. Marriage was inevitable one day, but she could not help but yearn for a love that transcended duty and social obligation. She wanted to find a love as genuine and heartfelt as the one her mother had read to her in those cherished stories. She day dreamed often about a love of her own...

"Genie, look!" Harry called out, using the sweet little nickname that only he had for her. "Look at this butterfly."

*Oh no!* Horror struck Genevieve as she followed her brother's voice to see him standing far closer to the stables than he should be. The stable men were currently breaking in a new horse, Midnight, who had a *very* excitable temperament. Trying her hardest not to panic, Genevieve slowly rose to her feet, swallowing hard so the nerves did not overwhelm her completely.

"That is wonderful, Harry," she said quietly, slightly trembling as she thought about the warnings the stable boys had given her. "But I think you should come here now."

Unfortunately Harry was not listening to her, he was far too consumed by whatever creature he was currently following. Genevieve's heart pounded as she heard a rustling in the stables. It might have been nothing, and she tried to convince herself that it absolutely was nothing, but she could not switch off the panic.

"Harry, please!" she yelled a little louder this time around. "Come back here."

But still he did not seem to hear her. Harry did not even hear the hooves crashing against the stables wall. He was so consumed with the butterfly that nothing else mattered. Genevieve could only watch in horror as the wild horse broke free from its tether.

The majestic beast, fueled by fear, reared up and bolted with explosive force, its eyes wild and frenzied, its hooves thundering like a relentless storm.

Genevieve's heart clenched as alarm surged within her. She knew the danger that loomed, the impending catastrophe that was unfolding before her eyes. Her protective instincts roared to the surface. She no longer cared about being quiet and careful, that was the least of her issues.

"Harry! Look out!" she screamed, her voice carrying the urgency of impending peril.

Her desperate cry, intended to be a life line, drew her brother's innocent gaze. Startled by her shout, Harry turned towards the commotion, his innocent eyes widening in surprise. Unbeknownst to him, he had stepped right into the path of the rampaging horse, a calamity he was unaware of. The butterfly had flown away, but Harry was no longer watching it.

In that heart wrenching moment, time seemed to stretch, the world blurring into a whirl wind of chaos and fear. Genevieve watched in horror as her brother, her responsibility, stepped directly into the charging animal's trajectory.

"No!" she cried out in agony as the collision happened right before her very eyes. It killed her to see the horse trample right over her brother as if he were not even there. "No, Harry."

She raced towards him, her heart threatening to explode from her rib cage because she was so anxious. Her eyes blurred with panic, this was a nightmare. But soon, after what felt like the longest run of her life, Genevieve reached her brother. Harry, miraculously alive, lay on the ground, his small frame bruised and battered. His leg was twisted at a terrible looking angle, but Genevieve was trying not to focus on that, because she was so grateful to see her brother breathing.

"Oh, Harry," she gasped as she brushed her fingers through her hair. "I will get a doctor immediately. You are going to be fine."

Genevieve's heart pounded, her breath caught in her throat, and she was eclipsed by guilt. She had tried to save her brother, but her shout had unwittingly drawn his attention to the approaching danger. The crushing weight of her unintended role in the accident burrowed deep within her, influencing every subsequent decision and emotion, and shaping her determination to protect Harry from harm's way at all costs.

Thankfully others inside the home, the manor's staff, had heard the commotion and raced outside to help Genevieve with her brother. Much as she wanted to be his soul protector, she was in too deep, drowning under the pressure of this. It was beyond her abilities. For now, other people were going to have to step in.

\*\*\*

Jonathan stood at the helm of the ship, his knuckles white as he gripped the wheel. The once soothing lull of the waves had transformed in to a relentless, growing menace. The decision he had made, one he had believed to be sound, now gnawed at him with relentless doubt. Others had warned him of an upcoming storm, but he had heard that warning before and it was all for nothing. The weather stayed calm, and the water barely moved.

Jonathan trusted his gut, and now he was starting to see that perhaps he should not have.

The ship groaned, a wounded creature in the grip of a merciless tempest. Water lashed the deck like a furious beast, showing no mercy to the vessel or its crew. Fear, like an icy vice, tightened in his chest as the cries of his crew rose around him. Each desperate voice felt like a blade, cutting deeper in to his resolve.

*What am I doing?* He thought sadly to himself. *What have I done?*

It was as if his whole life had started flashing before his very eyes as he tried to keep the ship steady, but the relentless roar of the tempestuous sea surrounding him seemed to mirror the tumultuous journey of his own life. As the waves crashed against the sides of the ship, threatening to overwhelm it, Jonathan's thoughts drifted back to the unexpected twist of fate that had brought him to this perilous position.

Jonathan Grantham had not been born with the weight of the dukedom upon his shoulders. It was his elder cousin who had been destined to inherit the title and the accompanying responsibilities. While his family held an esteemed place in the aristocracy, they were several steps removed from the direct line of succession, which afforded them a bit more freedom in their choices and pursuits.

Given this liberty, Jonathan's father had encouraged his son to follow a family tradition that was cherished for generations on his side — the tradition of the sea. Tales of naval adventures passed down through the generations had a profound impact on young Jonathan, instilling in him a deep sense of duty and a deep love for the vast, unpredictable ocean.

The sea had become his realm of adventure, where the ebb and flow of the tides matched the rhythm of his own life. But on this fateful voyage, as the ship moaned and the water lashed the deck, he could not help but question the decisions that had led him to this moment. At three and twenty years of age, he had ruined everything.

He felt like a fool, and he did not know how to make things right.

The weight of his command, the lives of his crew, and the decisions he had made gnawed at him with doubt and regret. Each desperate voice raised in cries for help felt like a dagger, slicing deeper into his resolve. The ship seemed to be cracking around him, mirroring the fragments of his own confidence that were falling apart.

"Get to safety!" someone yelled as the ship began to really splinter, and with it, fragments of Jonathan's once unwavering confidence shattered. Jonathan was not even sure who it was speaking, which made his chest ache. He knew all of these men well, they were his team and his confidants. Now he had no idea what on earth was happening around him. Nothing could be more terrifying to a ship's captain than that. "Abandon ship. It is every man for himself."

Those few who managed to scramble to safety were blurred figures in the chaos, but Jonathan's focus was consumed by the haunting echo of those he could not save. Not everyone managed to climb off the boat, the waves claimed them before they could save themselves. The sea, once his realm of adventure and exploration, now felt like a vast expanse of judgment. It offered no solace, only relentless retribution. The waves, which had once been his companions, now seemed determined to engulf him in their dark depths.

Amidst the chaos, one thought persisted, unrelenting in its torment: his role in this tragedy and whether he would ever find redemption. Guilt weighed down on him like a leaden anchor, and regret filled his lungs, making every breath a painful reminder of his choices. He did not even know if he would survive this, but one thing was for sure. If he did, it would be a day that haunted him for the rest of his existence. He would never be able to shake off what he had done here.

The tempest raged on, the ship continued to break apart, and the sea seemed insatiable in its fury. Jonathan clung to the wheel, a captain with a sinking vessel, haunted by his decisions, and tormented by the question of whether he could ever make amends for the lives lost on this tumultuous voyage.

# CHAPTER 1

*Present day,*
*Graftonshire, Winter...*

Genevieve's footsteps were silent on the plush carpet as she stepped into the family library, a sanctuary of knowledge and wisdom that had been her refuge throughout her life. The familiar scent of aged paper and polished mahogany enveloped her, a comforting embrace that never failed to soothe her restless spirit.

The library was a sanctuary of her family's history, a repository of tales and wisdom passed down through generations. As she skimmed her fingers over the titles, each spine whispered secrets and stories, their worn bindings holding a world of knowledge. The shelves were a testament to her ancestors' love for literature, a treasure trove of their collective wisdom.

However, amidst the well worn volumes and the comforting ambiance, one particular leather bound journal captured her attention. One she had not noticed before now. It lay nestled on a lower shelf, as though waiting for her to discover its hidden secrets. The journal, its pages yellowed with age, held an air of mystery that beckoned to her.

With delicate fingers and a racing pulse, Genevieve gently lifted the journal from its resting place. The leather cover, softened by time, seemed to pulse with the heartbeat of countless tales contained within. She carefully opened the journal and began to leaf through its pages, her eyes devouring the elegant script that adorned them.

It was clear that the journal was old, the ink fading but still legible. Genevieve's curiosity deepened as she read the name etched on the first page: *Lord Alan Ellsworth*. The name was familiar; Lord Allan was her grandfather whose life had been shrouded in mystery. Unfortunately, he had passed away before she was born so she never got to know him. But perhaps this was a time where she could finally get to understand him better.

The discovery sent a shiver down Genevieve's spine. It was as though Lord Alan's voice, long silenced by time, had whispered to her from the past, inviting her to unravel the mysteries hidden within the pages. Genevieve knew that this journal held the key to a deeper understanding of her family's history and the secrets that had been passed down through the generations. With a sense of determination and excitement, she settled into a comfortable chair, ready to embark on a journey through time and discover the hidden truths that lay within the journal's weathered pages.

Genevieve delicately turned the page of the old leather bound journal, its pages protesting softly as they unveiled the secret words hidden within. As she turned the first page with care, a yellowed letter, fragile with age, gently fell into her lap. It bore no specific addressee, as if it had been meant for anyone who dared to discover its contents.

*Treasure?* Genevieve thought to herself as she saw what appeared to be a map. *Buried here?*

The flowing script, written by her late grandfather, revealed a secret that had been buried in the depths of her family's history. Genevieve's heart quickened as she read his words, which hinted at an unsolved mystery, a treasure hidden within the very boundaries of Graftonshire itself. It was a treasure that had eluded generations, a puzzle waiting to be solved, and a legacy left behind by their ancestors. The sort of mystery that Genevieve had only thought occurred in stories before now, never in real life. But perhaps she was wrong.

The words on the weathered parchment were filled with riddles and half truths, evoking a flurry of emotions within Genevieve. Excitement coursed through her veins, the prospect of adventure beckoning with an irresistible charm. Doubt, too, gnawed at the edges of her excitement. Could this treasure be real, or was it merely a product of her grandfather's imagination? Was it simply a story that he had written to let time by-pass him, or was there more to it? She desperately wanted to unravel this mystery, and she felt an insatiable thirst for adventure welling up inside her.

It was the map that really caught Genevieve's attention. It was meticulously drawn and aged like fine wine. It revealed the landscape of Graftonshire and its surrounding areas, with cryptic markings and symbols hinting at the location of the hidden treasure. The map was a tantalizing puzzle, a key that could unlock the secrets of the past and lead to the elusive *treasure* that had remained hidden for centuries. If it were real.

*Oh, I so hope that this is real.*

Genevieve was immersed in the contents of the letter, the words etched in time by her late grandfather. As she followed the trail of clues and riddles with her fingers along the map, a bitter sweet memory surfaced, like a fragile petal carried by the winds of time. She thought about the horrible passing of her mother once more, a memory that threatened to overwhelm her every single time she thought of it.

But this time, instead of focusing on her mother's passing, she thought about the wonderful times they had as a family when she was still alive. She remembered once more the stories that her mother used to tell Harry and her. It was her mother who had often regaled Harry and her with bed time stories, filled with adventures and hidden treasures. With treasure maps based on their land, just like this one. With each story, her mother's eyes would twinkle, and her voice would carry a hint of mystery, as if she held secrets close to her heart.

*Did she know?* Genevieve thought to herself. It certainly felt like it at the time. Her mother had spun the story with such vivid detail that it had felt like a promise — a promise that one day they would uncover the hidden riches and embark on a grand adventure together.

Just as she brushed the tear away, a soft voice interrupted her musings. Genevieve turned her head, her eyes meeting those of her younger brother, Harry. He stood there, smiling at her, filling her with warmth and love, even though guilt tinged the edges of everything.

"Genevieve," he said, his voice a gentle and comforting presence. "What are you reading?"

She closed the letter, her heart still heavy with memories. "It's a letter from Grandfather," she replied, her voice filled with a mixture of excitement and nostalgia. "He left us a puzzle, Harry, a treasure to find. Do you remember the stories that Mother used to tell about the treasure of Graftonshire? I think she was telling us the truth, not stories."

Harry's eyes lit up with curiosity, the same youthful wonder she had seen in him as a child. Despite his limitations, caused by the accident that happened on that dreaded day, six years ago. Yet despite everything, he remained her steadfast companion, her confidante, and her source of strength.

"Come." She patted the seat beside her. "Sit with me."

Her heart was heavy with guilt, and the weight of a memory weighed her down, refusing to be ignored as Harry limped over to her with the leg that had never quite healed. She could not escape the memory of the heart wrenching day when Harry had been forever changed.

If only she had not called out to him when the wild horse broke free, if only she had not been distracted, if only she had done everything differently. Those thoughts, like a relentless storm, swirled within her, tormenting her with the *what ifs* and the burden of her actions. She could not escape the responsibility she felt for her brother's suffering, and it was a weight she would carry with her for the rest of her life.

But Harry did not look like he blamed his sister for anything as he took a seat beside her, right underneath their mother's portrait, which was their favorite place to be.

Genevieve and Harry's bond was evident in the silent exchange that found them both sitting in front of a portrait of their mother. The art work, radiant and filled with life, was a stark contrast to the void left in her wake. Her eyes in the portrait seemed to sparkle with the same mystery and wonder that had filled their childhood, that made Genevieve miss her painfully.

"It feels like she is still with us, does it not?" Harry said softly, breaking the silence that had hung between them.

Genevieve nodded, her voice equally soft as she replied, "Yes, it does. Her memory is a treasure, just like the one our grandfather wrote about."

"Remember the stories she used to tell us?" Genevieve began, a wistful smile gracing her lips.

Harry's eyes lit up with nostalgia. "The tales of adventures, hidden treasures, and faraway lands? I used to believe every word, and now it seems like that might be because some of what she told us was the truth."

Genevieve chuckled, "So did I. She had a way of making the ordinary seem extraordinary. You might be right, maybe because there was truth within it."

"She taught us to dream big, to believe in the impossible," Harry added. "And she always said that we were capable of achieving anything we set our minds to."

Genevieve's eyes welled with tears, but they were tears of love and gratitude. "Yes, she did. She taught us the power of love, of family, and of never giving up."

But she often wondered if her mother would still love her quite as much as she had if she had been alive when Harry had his accident. Would she have been outcast from the family because it was all her fault? Her father never treated her any differently, but because her mother was not around she would never know.

Genevieve wiped away a tear and turned to face her brother, a strange new determination surging through her. "We should find that hidden treasure, Harry. Not just for us, but for her. Like a promise we're making to our mother. She is not here anymore, but if she were, you know she would want us to do this."

"Do you think so?" Harry asked, but it was clear that he liked the idea by the way his eyes shone with determination. "If you think that this is something we must do, then I am fully in accord with you, Genevieve. We can honour Mother's memory and uncover the secrets our grandfather left behind. Who knows what we will discover about our family land along the way."

As they looked back at the radiant portrait of their mother, it felt as though her eyes held a knowing twinkle, as if she was watching over them with pride and love. The legacy of their mother's wisdom and love would guide them on their journey, reminding them of the strength that came from their shared bond and the enduring power of family, Genevieve was sure of it.

The tender moment shared by Genevieve and Harry was interrupted by the polite, measured voice of the butler, who had appeared at the library door. He cleared his throat and announced, "My Lady, Master Harry, Lady Eleanor and her parents have arrived."

Grateful for the distraction, Genevieve and Harry exchanged a quick, understanding glance before making their way out of the library to greet their relatives. Their cousin Eleanor and her parents were an exciting arrival, having journeyed to spend the winter with them at Graftonshire.

As they entered the grand foyer together, Genevieve's heart swelled with warmth at the sight of her cousin. Eleanor was a close confidante, and her arrival was a welcome addition to the household. Eleanor's parents, too, were cherished family members, and their presence brought an air of merriment and companionship to the grand estate. Elanor's mother, Caroline, was her mother's sister, so often had tales and memories to make Genevieve feel closer to the woman that she had lost.

Eleanor, her face alight with excitement, stepped forward and embraced Genevieve tightly. "Genevieve, Harry, it has been far too long! I have missed you both dearly."

Harry, despite his pronounced limp, moved forward to join the warm welcome. "Eleanor, we are delighted to have you here. It has been too quiet without your laughter echoing through the halls."

Their parents, with smiles that revealed their shared joy, joined the gathering. The family reunion was filled with laughter, embraces, and the promise of shared moments by the hearth during the coming winter. The library's secrets and the hidden treasure would have to wait, for the bonds of family and the warmth of their presence were a treasure of a different kind, one that Genevieve and Harry cherished beyond measure.

\*\*\*

The evening sun dipped below the horizon as the family gathered for dinner in the opulent dining room of Graftonshire. The soft glow of candle light cast a warm and inviting ambiance over the meal. Genevieve quickly decided to use this opportunity, with all of her family together, and she could not resist the urge to steer the conversation toward the rumored treasure of Graftonshire.

"Have you ever heard the tales, Eleanor?" Genevieve asked, her voice carrying an air of intrigue, hoping that everyone in the room would hear her. "The stories of hidden treasures, secret maps, and unsolved mysteries that have whispered through the halls of Graftonshire for generations?"

Eleanor, ever the romantic dreamer, leaned forward in her seat, her eyes sparkling with excitement. "Oh, I have heard the tales, Genevieve," she replied. "The stories are like something out of a fairy tale — a treasure chest filled with jewels, hidden beneath the ancient ruins, waiting for a brave soul to uncover it."

Harry, quickly catching on to what Genevieve was doing, nodded in agreement. "Yes, and the moonlit quests through the Grafton Moors, following cryptic clues to find the treasure, make for thrilling tales."

Their father, Lord Edward Ellsworth, a man of reason and intellect, regarded the conversation with a more skeptical eye. He spoke with a firm voice tinged with practicality. "My children, those are nothing more than myths and legends meant to entertain young minds. Graftonshire is rich in history, but there is no treasure waiting to be discovered. The stories are but fanciful tales created for the amusement of children. I have grown up listening to such stories myself. They do not mean a thing, do not get distracted by something that does not exist."

Genevieve could not help but feel a touch of disappointment at her father's dismissal. While she understood his perspective, the allure of the hidden treasure and the adventure it promised had always captured her imagination, and now that she had the letter with the clues, and the map in hand, she was not about to be deterred.

As the evening progressed, the conversation at the dinner table flowed in other directions, but Genevieve's thoughts remained firmly fixed on the treasure hunt that beckoned her. Her determination was unwavering, despite what her father had said, and she made a silent vow to herself that she would unravel this mystery, even if it meant going against her father's wishes. She could only hope that Harry was in agreement with her.

While her father was a man of reason and practicality, she had inherited her mother's spirit of adventure and seemingly her grandfather's love for the unknown. The tales of hidden treasures and moonlit quests had captured her imagination, and she could not let them go.

# CHAPTER 2

Darkness descended upon Jonathan, a suffocating shroud that enveloped him as he stood on the rain soaked deck of his ship. The tempest raged around him, rain lashing against his skin like a thousand needles, and the relentless fury of the storm threatened to toss him in to the abyss of the roiling sea.

The desperate cries of his men, those loyal souls who had followed his command, barely reached his ears over the deafening roar of the high winds. Their voices were like distant echoes in the maelstrom, cries of fear and desperation that mingled with the howling wind and crashing waves.

The weight of his choices, his decisions as the captain, bore down on him with unrelenting force. He had believed in the path he had chosen, had placed his trust in the fates of the sea, and now, they exacted a heavy toll.

But then, a chilling realization sliced through the turmoil — a harsh, unforgiving truth that threatened to consume him. His ship, the vessel that had been his command and his responsibility, would not survive this storm. It was a doomed voyage, and the sea, once his realm of adventure, now felt like a vast expanse of judgment. He knew what the outcome of this nightmare was going to be now because it had happened in real life a few years ago, but unfortunately there was not a thing he could do to change it. Much as he tied to reach out to the blurry figures surrounding him, they were always just out of reach. He wanted to keep them safe, but he did not have the ability to do so. He never had done, and he never would do.

As the water swarmed the deck and cries of his crew rose around him, a crushing weight of guilt and remorse burrowed deep within his chest. He felt responsible for the lives of his men, the brave souls who had followed him into the heart of the storm. The cyclone had claimed their ship, and he had led them into this treacherous journey. The hopelessness was just as suffocating as the water that kept crashing over him, whipping the air right out of his lungs. He was not sure what was crushing him down the hardest, this was too much to bear, he wanted to stop reliving it so he could get back to his life, but that never happened….

And then, as quickly as it had come... silence descended.

The chaos of the high seas was replaced by an eerie stillness, a stark contrast to the fury that had reigned moments before. The ship was gone, the sea had claimed it, and the guilt and regret that had filled his heart were now an unending abyss of sorrow.

Jonathan stood on a now empty deck, drenched and battered, a captain who had lost his ship and the men who had entrusted their lives to him. In the aftermath of the nightmare, he was left to grapple with the haunting question of whether he would ever find redemption for the choices he had made...

Suddenly, Jonathan awoke, gasping for breath as his heart pounded in the stillness of his bed chamber. The remnants of the nightmare clung to him like a shroud, the harrowing images refusing to fade from his mind. Sweat clung to his forehead, a tangible reminder of the intensity of the dreams that had tormented his sleep.

Rising to his feet and dragging his aching heavy body along, he pushed the heavy drapes aside. Jonathan was greeted by the serene calm of the dawn over Grafton Moors. The sun light filtered through the window, casting a warm, gentle glow across the room. It was a stark contrast to the nightmarish dark storm that had just haunted his dreams. But the fact that this was his reality did not bring him any comfort. The nightmares were imprinted in his brain as memories from the past, and there was truly no escaping that.

It had been only two weeks since his mother, Rosalind and he arrived at Graftonshire, a place that had been both familiar and foreign to him. In the wake of an unforeseen inheritance, he had assumed a new role and a new title as the Duke of Graftonshire, a position he had never anticipated.

The transition had been swift and unexpected, thrusting him into the responsibilities and duties of a title he had never sought. The weight of his new role had brought with it a sense of unease, and the nightmares that plagued his sleep were a reflection of the turmoil that churned within him.

He did not know what to do with this newfound responsibility. The title had been meant for his cousin, Miles, the rightful heir. The future of Graftonshire had been planned differently, and Jonathan had been content with that. He had embarked on a path of his own, choosing a life in the navy and to follow his own heart.

But fate had taken a cruel twist. Miles had met a tragic end in a carriage accident, and the title of the dukedom, with all its responsibilities, had unexpectedly fallen to Jonathan. It was a burden he never sought, a role he hadn't prepared for, and it left him grappling with a sense of not belonging.

Jonathan could not help but wonder if he would ever find his place as the Duke of Graftonshire, or if he would forever feel like an imposter in a role that was never meant to be his. The uncertainty gnawed at him even now as he sat on the edge of his bed, the dawn's light continuing to stream into the room, offering some semblance of calm and clarity.

With a deep breath, he resolved to face the challenges that lay ahead. He could not change the past, much as he wanted to, but he could determine his future. The calm dawn of Graftonshire was a fresh start, a chance to embrace the new role that destiny had thrust upon him, if he could find a way.

As he began to dress, the weight of the unforeseen change in his life's direction pressed upon him like a leaden cloak. Each article of clothing he donned served as a stark reminder of the transformation that had occurred in his life. For his mother's sake, he would have to do what he could to make the best of it though. She expected a lot from him, and since he was not sure that he had ever been able to make her proud before, now he truly wanted to.

Breakfast in the elegant drawing room of Graftonshire was a refined affair, bathed in the soft light of morning. Jonathan, now fully attired, sat at the head of the table, his thoughts still lingering on the unexpected twists of his life. As he quietly sipped his tea, his cousin Agatha, the Duchess of Graftonshire and sister to the late Miles, brimmed with enthusiasm beside him.

"Jonathan, my dear cousin," Agatha bubbled with infectious excitement, her eyes sparkling with energy. "I have been giving it much thought, and I believe it is time that we celebrate your recent ascension to the title of Duke of Graftonshire with a grand ball!" The suggestion hung in the air, and the room seemed to come alive with Agatha's vivacious spirit. "It could be the highlight of the season's social events, a spectacle that would draw the aristocracy from near and far to Graftonshire. My brother always wanted our home town to be more central to the social scene, but with the distance from London he did not think it possible. I would like to do this in his honour also."

Jonathan regarded his cousin with a mixture of surprise and gratitude. Her enthusiasm was a stark contrast to his own apprehension about his new role. Her suggestion offered a glimmer of light in the midst of the uncertainty that had settled over him. Plus, she wanted to do this for Miles and that was something Jonathan could not push to one side. He wanted to honor Miles as well, but secretly he did agree with Miles. It was too far from London to ever *really* be a part of the ton's social life. But that did not mean they should not try.

"It is a marvelous idea, Agatha," he replied with a smile, feeling a sense of warmth in her presence. "A grand ball to mark this new chapter in my life — it would be an honour."

Agatha beamed, her enthusiasm undiminished. "I knew you would see the appeal, Jonathan. The ball will be a splendid affair, and I shall take charge of all the arrangements. It will be the talk of the season, a night to remember."

Perhaps the grand ball would be a celebration of his newfound title, a chance to step into his new role with confidence and grace. As the conversation continued, the prospect of the grand ball loomed ahead, offering a glimmer of hope and a sense of purpose in the midst of the uncertainties that had marked his recent ascension to the title of Duke of Graftonshire.

As Agatha and Jonathan's mother engaged in animated discussion about the estate and the upcoming festivities, Jonathan sat at the table, though his physical presence was merely a formality. The grand ball was a subject of great enthusiasm for both women, their voices filled with energy and anticipation, but their conversation reached him as if from a great distance. He felt himself slipping away mentally from what was happening around him. He would be expected to attend the ball, but that was all. He did no need to join in with the arrangements. For now, he could try and adjust to himself as best as he could...

\*\*\*

Later that day, Jonathan found solace in his study, the room where he often retreated to sketch scenes of the ocean. This was the closest that he could get to the sea these days, and while it was not the same as actually being out on the ocean, this was lovely. Much better than worrying any longer about everything that he could not change. The familiar sound of charcoal on paper was a comforting presence, allowing him to lose himself in the art, if only for a while.

As he focused on capturing the waves and the call of the sea on paper, a sense of tranquility washed over him. The study, adorned with nautical charts and sketches of ships, was a sanctuary where he could temporarily escape the weight of his new role as the Duke of Graftonshire. It was where he could recall what his life used to be like, before the terrible day when everything went awry and his life was irrevocably upended. The day of the storm...

But the soothing rhythm of sketching was disrupted when the butler entered the room, a formal expression on his face. "Your Grace, there is a visitor to see you," he announced.

Jonathan looked up, curiosity piqued. He could not imagine who would seek him out on this particular day.

The butler continued, "It's Captain Lucas Beaumont, My Lord. He has arrived to spend the winter at Graftonshire."

A rush of warmth and genuine surprise flooded Jonathan. Lucas was not just a visitor but a dear friend, his closest confidant from his naval days. One of the only people that could make him smile during this very difficult time in his life.

"Show him in, please," Jonathan said with enthusiasm as he placed his sketching to one side.

Moments later, the study door swung open, and there, with an exuberant smile, stood Captain Lucas Beaumont. His arrival was a breath of fresh air, a welcome interruption to the solitude that had enveloped Jonathan.

They greeted each other warmly, shaking hands with the familiarity of old friends. "Lucas, it has been too long," Jonathan said with a grin.

"Indeed, my friend," Lucas replied, a twinkle in his eye. "I could not stay away from Graftonshire for too long. How have you been adjusting to your newfound title, Duke Jonathan?"

"I am not adjusting to it yet," Jonathan laughed. "And I do not know if I will ever be able to.

Jonathan's shoulders relaxed as they settled into comfortable chairs, sharing a drink brought to them by the butler. The room was filled with shared stories, and their laughter echoed through the space. They reminisced about their adventures at sea, the near misses, and the daring escapades that had forged a bond stronger than any anchor chain.

Jonathan leaned back in his chair, a grin playing on his lips. "Do you remember that bout of bad weather off the coast of Gibraltar?" he asked.

Lucas chuckled, his eyes reflecting the memories. "Ah, how could I forget? The waves were like mountains, and the wind howled like a banshee. But we navigated through it quite well. I believe that assisted us in forming the tight bond that we share today."

"Indeed," Jonathan replied, his gaze fixed on a distant point as he relived the moment. "I thought we were done for, but you never lost your composure. Your calm under pressure saved us that day." It was a calm he wished he could also have had on the day the storm ruined everything.

As they shared these tales and more, the weight of Jonathan's new title as the Duke of Graftonshire seemed to melt away. In the presence of his old friend, he was once again Captain Jonathan Grantham, a man of the sea, unburdened by the aristocratic responsibilities that had been thrust upon him. The laughter and camaraderie they had shared throughout their voyages remained, a testament to the enduring strength of their friendship.

Lucas was a man of adventure, and his tales of far off lands and daring escapades were a reminder of the world beyond the estate's boundaries. His presence was a reminder of the camaraderie and brotherhood that had once been a defining part of Jonathan's life. It reminded him of how things used to be.

As they clinked glasses, Jonathan could not help but feel a renewed sense of purpose and a rekindling of the adventurous spirit that had been temporarily obscured by the responsibilities of his title. The arrival of his best friend was a timely and heartwarming reminder that life could still hold moments of joy and exhilaration, even amidst the unexpected twists of fate.

# CHAPTER 3

Genevieve lay in her bed chamber, the first rays of dawn softly creeping through the drapes. It was a still, quiet moment, and she could not shake the thoughts that had been haunting her since the discovery of her grandfather's letter. Its enigmatic message had drawn her in, and it now occupied her thoughts in the hushed hours of morning. Actually it seemed to occupy all of her thoughts. She could not stop thinking about it. The adventure was calling to her, no matter what she did.

Just as Genevieve rose to her feet, her maid, Madeline, entered the room, her face illuminated by a warm smile. "Good morning, Lady Genevieve," she greeted with a curtsy.

Genevieve returned the smile. "Good morning, Madeline. It does look like a lovely day today. The sun is starting to shine."

Madeline approached Genevieve, her nimble fingers working deftly as she assisted her with getting dressed. The gown chosen for the day was a lovely one. It was made of silk, a soft shade of periwinkle that accentuated Genevieve's fair complexion.

But despite everything, Genevieve's mind remained consumed by the words and the mysteries contained within that aged piece of parchment. She could hardly focus on the dress she was wearing when she was all but consumed with the vision of hidden treasures and the promise of adventure that had taken root in her imagination, and it seemed that the enigma of the letter held both the allure and confounding enigma of a riddle.

Genevieve could not help but be entranced by the possibilities that the letter presented. Her grandfather, a man of intellect and imagination according to all the stories that she had been told about him over the years, had left her with a legacy of wonder and curiosity. The tales of secrets concealed within Graftonshire's boundaries, the ancient ruins, and the treasure waiting to be uncovered were like echoes of a by gone era, whispers from the past that beckoned to her.

As Madeline assisted her in fastening the intricate buttons of her gown, Genevieve's thoughts continued to drift. Everything that lay ahead filled her mind, and she could almost feel the wind on her face as she explored the hidden corners of her family's estate.

She knew that the path she was contemplating was not without challenges and uncertainties. It would take courage and determination to unravel the mysteries of her grandfather's letter and map. But as she looked at herself in the mirror, she saw a reflection of a woman determined to embrace the legacy left by her ancestors and to follow the call of adventure. The call that she was increasingly certain her mother wanted her to follow.

"Thank you," she muttered to Madeline once she was dressed and her hair brushed and styled. "You have been a wonderful help this morning."

"Is there anything else that I can help you with, Lady Genevieve?"

"No, I am fine, thank you very much. I shall go to breakfast now."

Entering the elegant dining room for breakfast, Genevieve was enveloped by the excited chatter of her family. Their voices filled the air, buzzing with anticipation and enthusiasm for an upcoming grand ball in Graftonshire, that she had not yet heard of.

"There is going to be a dance?" she asked as she lowered herself in to her seat.

"Oh yes," her aunt, Caroline replied happily. "To celebrate the new Duke of Graftonshire's ascension."

"Oh... I see." Genevieve had never had any interaction with the previous duke, but she knew his death in a carriage accident had been a terrible one. "There is a new duke?"

"I have heard a lot about it," Eleanor interjected excitedly. "They say he is of average height, but with broad shoulders that make him quite imposing. His hair is ash blond, and his eyes are a striking shade of green. I have heard he possesses the sort of handsome features that could make any lady's heart flutter. How very exciting."

"I see..." Genevieve still was not sure how to take this unexpected news. Not that it would have much of an impact on her life, she supposed.

Eleanor, always the romantic, could not resist adding her own embellishments. "They say he is a true gentleman, Genevieve, with a voice as smooth as honey. Perhaps on the night of the ball, you will have the pleasure of hearing it."

A faint blush crept in to Genevieve's cheeks as she tried to suppress a smile. The idea of the Duke's voice, as described by her cousin, did pique her interest. Though she had her reservations about her future, there was no harm in enjoying a little intrigue at the ball.

Eleanor and her mother, Caroline, engaged in animated conversations about the Duke, their speculations and musings on his charm, which prompted soft laughter from the women. Genevieve could not help but smile at their amusement, her heart warmed by the easy camaraderie between mother and daughter. Although of course it made her miss her own mother too. Would she be alongside the women also gossiping about the duke and how alluring he might be?

But as she forced that smile, refusing to show any sadness that might be swirling within her, an inner restlessness tugged at her, an irresistible pull that drew her attention to the window and the world beyond. The room was alive with excitement, but she could not help feeling a yearning for the boundless adventures that awaited her outside those walls.

The grand ball and the social gatherings of the ton were important, and she understood their significance in her family's eyes. They were part of the life she had been raised to lead, a life of responsibilities and expectations. But deep down, there was a part of her that longed for something more, something beyond the confines of societal norms. The world was vast, and her grandfather's letter had shown her a glimpse of the adventures that waited. The vision of hidden treasures was a call that she could not ignore.

After breakfast, when Eleanor and her mother, Lady Caroline, retreated to the drawing room for their embroidery, Genevieve found herself declining their invitation to join. She could not resist the attraction of adventure any longer. The call of the unknown was too powerful to ignore. She would not be able to sit still any longer with the map in her mind.

With haste, she made her way to her bedchamber, where a thick winter cloak and gloves awaited her. The knowledge she had gained from her grandfather's letter had pointed her towards the Seabrook Ruins, perched on the cliffs of Graftonshire. At least, that was what she had gleaned from the clues so far. She could only hope that she was right. The promise of a hidden treasure and the mysteries that awaited were impossible to resist.

Without pause, Genevieve snuck back through the hallways of her home, hoping not to see anyone, and she stepped outside, greeted by the invigorating chill of the winter air. Her heart raced as she was filled with excitement and anticipation. She could not help but feel a sense of exhilaration as she began to make her way towards the ruins.

However, as she ventured further from the safety of her family's estate, a familiar voice called out to her, stopping her in her tracks. It was Harry whose concerned gaze met hers. He had become protective and caring of Genevieve, especially since their mother's death and the accident that had left him with a limp. The older her grew up, the more protective over her he became. They had become mutual pillars of support in each other's lives.

His suspicion was evident as he looked at Genevieve, guessing her intentions. With a firm but gentle tone, he started. "Genevieve, you can not embark on this adventure alone. It would be improper, and I worry for your safety. Let me accompany you, as a brother should. We shall face the unknown together, just as we discussed in the library. This is not something that Mother would wish for you to do alone, you know that."

Genevieve, torn between her desire for independence and her love for her brother, hesitated for a moment. She knew that Harry's presence would bring a sense of security, and his company was a comfort she could not deny. With a reluctant but appreciative smile, she nodded in agreement. He was right, their mother would have wanted this to be something that they did together, to bring them closer. Family was so very important to her.

"Very well, Harry," she said, "we shall embark on this adventure together, as we always have. But remember, this journey is not without its dangers and uncertainties. We must be cautious and prepared for the unknown."

"I know as much." Harry rolled his eyes and laughed. "That is why I wish to come with you. It might be treacherous, but I am sure it shall also be fun."

As Genevieve and Harry walked towards the Seabrook Ruins, her heart was heavy with concern. She could not help but observe her brother's pace faltering, his limp growing more noticeable with each step. Guilt washed over her like a relentless tide, threatening to engulf her. The weight of her brother's struggles, potentially exacerbated by her quest for adventure, pierced her heart. She did not ever wish to be the person who caused him *more* pain. She knew that she had done enough.

Unable to bear the thought of Harry's discomfort, she came to a halt and turned to face him. The unspoken tension between them was palpable, and their eyes met in a silent stand off. The determination in Genevieve's gaze was matched by Harry's reluctance to concede. He seemed to already know what she was going to say, which meant she was likely correct in saying it. He did not like taking care of himself when it affected other people, even if that other person was his very own sister.

"Harry," she implored, her voice filled with a mixture of love and concern. "You should rest. Your comfort is of utmost importance to me. There is a rock just there," she said, pointing to a nearby boulder. "Please, sit down and catch your breath. Just for a few minutes."

"I do not wish to slow you down. That is not why I came with you."

"I will rest with you," Genevieve insisted. "I am tired also. We can take a moment to sit down, and maybe look over the map some more."

Harry grew impatient with his sister, likely caused by the pain he was feeling. "Would it not make more sense to view the map once we arrive? I do not see the point in wasting time looking at it now when we are not too far away."

But Genevieve could also be stubborn. She was not going to allow this to continue. "I am resting. You do whatever you wish, but I would like to see the map and the clues here. I refuse to take another step until I have done so.

Reluctantly, and because she left him no choice in the matter, Harry finally conceded to Genevieve's wishes. He sighed and moved toward the indicated rock, his eyes lingering on his sister. Genevieve watched him closely, her heart heavy with the magnitude of her mission and the weight of how this might impact Harry. She wanted it be to something fun that they shared, not something that made his life any harder than it already was. That was the last thing she wanted.

As Harry settled on the rock and leaned against it, Genevieve could not help but feel a mixture of gratitude for his presence and guilt for the burdens he bore. She knew that her quest for adventure had the potential to make his struggles more pronounced, and that thought weighed heavily on her.

Would this be worth it in the end? Or was she about to make everything so much worse?

# CHAPTER 4

During breakfast, the air was thick with Agatha's palpable enthusiasm as she regaled the family with tales of the Duke and Duchess of Cavendale, who were soon to be guests at the grand ball being held in Jonathan's honor. Her eyes sparkled with anticipation as she spoke.

"Oh, the Cavendales are truly a splendid family," Agatha continued, her voice filled with admiration. "The Duke and Duchess have always been such dear friends of ours, and their daughter, Lady Isabella, is a vision of grace and beauty. She's not only charming but also well educated, and her demeanour is truly befitting of a lady of her stature."

As Agatha's conversation continued, the undertones became more pronounced. She spoke of Lady Isabella's accomplishments, her education, and her grace with a certain emphasis that suggested she thought her to be a potential match for Jonathan. The unspoken expectations were clear — the future Duke of Graftonshire should consider Lady Isabella as a suitable companion, which was *not* what he had been planning on at all. He had not even thought about looking for love, not even for a second.

These implications weighed on Jonathan's mind, casting a shadow over the breakfast table. The idea of a predetermined match, arranged for the sake of societal expectations and the continuation of the Graftonshire name, left him feeling uneasy.

Thoughts of commitment and love had always seemed distant and elusive to him. His life had been defined by the sea, by the unpredictability of naval adventures and the thrill of discovery. The newfound responsibilities of his unexpected dukedom, along with the pressure to choose a future Duchess, left him with a sense of restlessness and discomfort that he did not know what to do with. Jonathan could not help but feel as though his destiny was being decided by others. The weight of tradition and the expectations of society seemed to close in around him, and the path he was meant to follow felt increasingly uncertain and daunting. The idea of love, commitment, and that sort of future with a family at his side seemed distant and unsettling, like an unfamiliar shore on a dark and stormy night.

As the conversation at the breakfast table continued, Jonathan found himself drifting in to the recesses of his own thoughts. The mention of Lady Isabella and the expectations that came with his title had brought forth memories of the harrowing voyage, one that he had long tried to bury but that always found a way to recur no matter what.

The faces of his crew, the ones who had sailed with him into the unforgiving sea, resurfaced in his mind. The memories of the ship groaning under the weight of the storm, the waves crashing against the deck, and the cries of his men echoed in his ears, getting louder with every passing second. When this happened, Jonathan was often surprised that no one else could hear the same yells as he did. He had been a leader, a captain entrusted with their lives, and the guilt of the choices he had made weighed heavily on his conscience.

People had died during that voyage, their lives sacrificed to the merciless sea. Their faces, the ones he had looked into as they clung to hope, haunted his dreams. The weight of their loss was a burden he had carried for years, and it had left him with a deep sense of guilt and responsibility. One that he was never going to overcome.

He loved those men like they were family, and he had managed to destroy them. That was something he would never do again. He had silently swore off the possibility of opening his heart again to anyone, ever. The scars of the past were still too fresh, the memories of that doomed voyage too vivid. The idea of love, of allowing someone to become a part of his life, was a prospect that seemed fraught with danger and pain. It scared him and caused a painful tension in his shoulders. He did not know if he could handle it.

Jonathan had become emotionally guarded, determined to protect himself from the vulnerability of opening his heart. The experiences of the past had taught him that love could be as treacherous as the stormy seas, and he was not willing to risk further heartache.

But he knew that he could not say that to his mother, who was smiling at him as if his future lay out before him. "What do you think, Jonathan? She sounds quite lovely."

"Mother, I have not yet met the young lady," he said, choosing his words carefully. " I hope you will allow me some time to adjust to my new role. I am sure that Lady Isabella is a delightful young lady, but I must admit that my heart is not entirely set on marriage at the moment."

Lady Rosalind's face showed a mixture of understanding and concern. She had always been supportive of her son's dreams, but now, the weight of the dukedom pressed heavily upon them both. Jonathan knew that she wanted to make sure that they did the right thing to keep them in with society, even if it was not something that either of them had prepared for.

"Jonathan, I only want what is best for you and our family," she said with a gentle sigh. "Consider the future, but do not close your heart off entirely. Love has a way of surprising us when we least expect it. If Agatha thinks that this woman might be the best fit for you, then you should listen to her."

Jonathan nodded, acknowledging his mother's wisdom. The idea of love seemed distant and unsettling in the face of his new responsibilities, but he could not deny the truth in her words. He knew that his cousin had his best interests at heart as well, but that did not mean he was going to immediately agree with everything that she said.

After breakfast, with the weight of the morning's conversation still lingering in his mind, Jonathan found himself seeking refuge in a familiar and comforting activity. He knew that a horseback ride, with the wind in his hair and the rhythmic sound of hooves against the ground, had always been a source of solace for him. He proposed the idea to Captain Lucas Beaumont, his best friend and confidant. Lucas, always ready for adventure, readily agreed, and they made their way to the stables.

As they mounted their horses and set off on the ride, the vastness of Graftonshire unfurled around them. The landscape was a breathtaking vista of rolling hills, lush meadows, and the sparkling waters of the River Lox. It was a place of natural beauty, untouched by the burdens of society and expectations. Jonathan had to admit that he did love his new surroundings, even if this was not where he expected to end up.

The rhythmic sound of hooves against the ground, the steady beat of their horses' hearts, and the stunning scenery provided a brief but much needed escape from the complexities of his new life as the Duke of Graftonshire. For a fleeting moment, Jonathan felt a sense of rejuvenation, as if the worries and responsibilities that had plagued him could be temporarily set aside.

As he rode alongside Lucas, the weight of the world seemed to lift, and for that brief interlude, Jonathan was able to find a sense of peace and clarity. The vastness of Graftonshire, with its untamed beauty, was a testament to the enduring allure of nature, a place where he could momentarily escape the expectations and pressures of his new role.

As they rode, Lucas filled the silences that Jonathan could not bear to speak through. Always the raconteur, he regaled Jonathan with stories of his past adventures traveling around the world. With each story, their shared laughter rang out, filling the morning air with a sense of joy and lightness. It was a wonderful break from everything that Jonathan was going through.

But he could not break away from it forever, so eventually they rode home. As they made their way back to Grafton Estate, the morning sun casting a warm glow over the landscape, Jonathan could not help but notice a hint of concern in Lucas's demeanor. His best friend's brow was furrowed, and there was a contemplative look in his eyes.

They dismounted their horses, and stood by the stables for a moment, until Lucas finally spoke, his words reflecting the wisdom of their years of friendship.

"Jonathan," Lucas began, his tone gentle yet earnest, "I have known you for a long time, and I have seen the weight of the past bear down on you. I understand the sorrow you carry, and I will not pretend to know the depths of it. But I also believe that it should not define your future."

Jonathan, grateful for Lucas's understanding and the bond they shared, listened intently. He knew that Lucas was addressing the unspoken reservations Jonathan held about love and commitment. He might not have been addressing it directly, but the meaning was clear regardless.

Lucas continued, "We can not change the past, my friend, but we can choose how we move forward. Do not let the sorrows of yesterday hold you back from the possibilities of tomorrow. There might be a brighter future waiting for you, one that you will not see if you keep your heart closed off."

Gratitude washed over Jonathan, not only for Lucas's understanding but for the gentle encouragement that his friend had offered. It was a reminder that he was not alone in his journey, that he had someone who believed in him and his capacity for growth and change.

"I know that you are right, Lucas," Jonathan replied with a smile. "And I appreciate what you are saying to me. I will definitely consider your words."

"Shall we go inside?"

Jonathan almost agreed, but at the last moment he changed his mind. He felt an inexplicable pull towards solitude and wished for more time alone. "I think I shall ride for a little while longer. Then I will join you."

Lucas nodded and shook his hand, before handing his horse to a stable boy and heading inside. Jonathan remounted his stead and rode towards the Seabrook Ruins, the ancient site with its stories embedded in every stone. It had always been a place of solace for him ever since he arrived in Graftonshire, a sanctuary where the weight of the world seemed to fade away.

Once he reached the cliffs overlooking the sea, the allure of the vast, boundless ocean drew him in. He dismounted, with his sketch book and pencil in hand, which he took with him everywhere, and approached the edge. The view before him was a breathtaking juxtaposition of calm yet tumultuous waves crashing against the steadfast ruins.

As his pencil danced across the page, capturing the essence of the sea and the ruins, Jonathan found himself lost in the world of his art. The burdens of his title, the looming ball, and the weight of societal expectations all seemed to recede into the background. In this moment, it was just Jonathan, his sketch book, and the infinite embrace of the sea.

The sound of the waves crashing against the cliffs, the feel of the cool breeze against his skin, and the rhythmic movement of his pencil brought a sense of tranquility that he had been yearning for all morning. The act of creating art, of capturing the beauty of the world around him, was a form of escape, a way to momentarily distance himself from his troubles.

In this solitary moment, Jonathan felt a sense of peace and freedom that had been elusive since he had become the Duke of Graftonshire. The world was reduced to the lines and shades on his sketch book, and the worries of the future seemed distant and inconsequential. For a while, he allowed himself to be lost in his art, savoring the serenity of the moment and finding solace in the embrace of the sea. It was a reminder that, amidst the responsibilities and expectations, there were still moments of respite and beauty to be found in the world.

# CHAPTER 5

Genevieve's heart sank as Harry looked at her with a mixture of concern and understanding. She already knew what he was going to say, before he even spoke.

"Go on, Genevieve," Harry said with a resigned smile. "I can not keep up with you, and I do not want to be a burden. Just be careful and stay safe."

She nodded, her heart heavy with the knowledge that this was for the best, even if it was hard. "I promise, Harry. I shall be cautious. I will not be long, and I will meet you back here."

With a final glance, Genevieve continued her journey towards her destination. The Seabrook Ruins loomed ahead, their ancient stones standing as silent sentinels, their stories echoing through the ages. The sight of the ruins beckoned Genevieve closer, their enigmatic past drawing her in like a siren's song. Each step she took towards them pulsed with a blend of thrill and uncertainty, her heart's rapid beat perfectly in sync with her determined foot steps.

As she approached the ruins, her grandfather's enigmatic words replayed in her head like a haunting melody. The cryptic letter and the map she had found had opened a door to a world of mysteries and hidden treasures. It was a riddle she was set on deciphering, an adventure waiting to be embarked upon.

The wind whispered through the cracks in the ancient stones, and the scent of the sea filled the air. It was a place where history and mystery converged, where the past and the present coexisted. Genevieve could not help but feel that she was on the cusp of a grand discovery, that the secrets hidden within these ruins were waiting to be unveiled. Excitement coursed through her veins as she walked, Genevieve had never felt quite as alive as she did at this moment.

As she approached the heart of the ruins, her gaze was drawn to a particular stone with weathered carvings. It was as if the stones themselves were eager to share their tales, to unravel the mysteries that had been buried for centuries. The weight of her grandfather's legacy and the promise of adventure infused every step with purpose and determination.

In that moment, amidst the ancient stones and the stories that seemed to seep from the very ground, Genevieve felt a profound connection to her family's history and a sense of destiny. She was determined to unlock the secrets that had been concealed for years, to follow in the footsteps of her grandfather, and to embrace the unknown with courage and curiosity. She was not even considering the possibility that she might find nothing. That was not an option. That was why she worked so hard internally to unravel the words and symbols that she had been thinking of ever since she first found the letter.

She could not wait to unlock the first clue and to find out what it all meant. But the land itself seemed to have its own intentions. An aggressive gust, nearly retaliatory, tore at her, yanking her cloak and spiriting away her bonnet. Genevieve's breath caught as she witnessed her bonnet, a precious memento from Harry, dance perilously near the cliff, the angry waves threatening beneath.

The sudden ferocity of the wind took her by surprise, and for a moment, she felt as if nature itself was challenging her quest. The elements, the very soul of Graftonshire, seemed to have a will of their own, as if they were testing her determination and resolve.

She could see her bonnet, a delicate and cherished keepsake, carried by the tempestuous winds towards the edge of the cliff. Panic surged within her, not for the loss of the material possession but for what it represented — Harry's love and her promise to protect it.

Without a second thought, Genevieve rushed towards the cliff's edge, her heart pounding with a mixture of fear and determination. The land, the ruins, and the sea blurred around her as she focused all her energy on reaching her bonnet before it succumbed to the waves.

The wind continued to buffet her, but Genevieve's determination was unwavering. With each step closer to the edge, the precipice that separated her from her precious bonnet seemed to grow more daunting. The waves roared below, a reminder of the peril that awaited her.

As she reached the very edge, her fingers stretching towards the dancing bonnet, the world seemed to hold its breath. The bonnet teetered on the brink of the cliff, perilously close to being lost to the tumultuous sea.

As hope seemed to wane, a figure emerged from the ruins' shadow. Genevieve watched, astounded, as he moved with a grace that contradicted the surrounding chaos. In a moment that felt almost magical, he seized her bonnet just as it teetered on the brink of being lost to the sea forever.

Her heart raced as the figure faced her, the bonnet safely in his grasp. It was a surreal and unexpected turn of events, and Genevieve could not help but feel a rush of gratitude and relief. The solitude she had felt, the sense of being alone in her quest, was suddenly shattered.

Their gaze entwined, an unspoken understanding passing between them amidst the turbulent setting. The man who had come to her aid was a stranger, but in that moment, he felt like a guardian angel, a mysterious presence who had stepped in when all seemed lost.

Warmth flooded Genevieve's cheeks, and she became hyper aware of the electricity in the space between them. The wind still raged, the sea continued its relentless dance with the cliffs, but in that suspended moment, it was as if time had slowed. There was a connection, a bond that transcended words and introductions. It was strange, not a sensation she had ever experienced before. Genevieve's heart swelled with gratitude, and she offered a smile, her eyes reflecting the depths of her appreciation.

The mysterious figure handed Genevieve her bonnet, and her heart fluttered with a mix of emotions. She watched in awe as the stranger, whose identity remained shrouded in the cloak of the sea sprayed air, revealed himself in the dimming light.

His silhouette was etched against the backdrop of the tempestuous sea, and Genevieve could not help but notice the remarkable figure before her. He stood with an air of confident strength, his shoulders broad and squared, as if the ocean's tumultuous waves had no power over him. His ash blond hair glistened with rain drops, tousled by the salty breeze. Piercing green eyes, like shards of emerald, met her gaze, and their intensity drew her in.

Genevieve's heartbeat quickened as she tried to make sense of this captivating encounter. Who was this enigmatic stranger who had saved her bonnet from the relentless sea? His presence was an enigma wrapped in intrigue, and she was both intrigued and captivated by him.

Unsure of what to say, she stammered, "Thank you. You... you saved my bonnet. I am Lady Genevieve Ellsworth."

His voice was as compelling as his appearance, deep and resonant, as he replied, "A pleasure to meet you, Miss Ellsworth. I am Jonathan Grantham, the new Duke of Graftonshire."

Jonathan Grantham — the name resonated in her mind. She had not expected the new Duke to be so young and handsome, having pictured an older, more conventional nobleman. Meeting him here, on the cliffs of Graftonshire, was entirely unexpected.

The electrifying tension between them was palpable, an unspoken connection that lingered in the salty air. Genevieve was drawn to his eyes, and the world seemed to blur around them. In that fleeting instant, amidst the storm's fury, she felt the stirrings of something she could not quite define.

Her heart raced, not only from the near loss of her bonnet but from the undeniable attraction she felt for the stranger who had emerged from the shadowy ruins. The wind-swept cliffs, the crashing waves, and the lingering eye contact all added to the potent cocktail of emotions that enveloped them.

Her attention broke when her foot caught on a slippery, moss covered stone. Panic surged through her as the world around her blurred, and a terrified cry involuntarily left her lips. In that heart stopping moment, it felt as though the ground had shifted beneath her, threatening to send her tumbling into the abyss.

But just as quickly as the fear came, she felt strong arms wrap around her, yanking her away from the precipice and ensuring her safety. Her heart continued to race, not only from the near fall but also from the sudden and unexpected proximity to the man she had just met who had come to her aid.

Genevieve's breaths came in ragged gasps as she clung to the edge of the cliff, her eyes wide with a mixture of fear and relief. The man's arms around her were a life line, a reassuring presence that had saved her from a potentially disastrous fall.

As the initial shock began to subside, she became acutely aware of the duke's closeness. She could feel the warmth of his breath against her cheek, and the steady beat of his heart seemed to echo in the silence that enveloped them. It was an intimate and electrifying moment, a connection formed in the face of danger.

Their eyes met, and in that unspoken exchange, Genevieve's world spiraled into a whirl wind of emotions. She felt a potent mixture of fear, relief, and a deep sense of gratitude. The storm tossed sea had almost claimed her, and yet, in the most unexpected of moments, the new Duke of Graftonshire had become her anchor, holding her steady on the precipice of danger.

His firm grip on her was unlike any touch she had ever experienced. It was not the chaste and formal contact of a ballroom dance or a gloved hand offered in greeting. Instead, it was a touch of raw, visceral intensity that sent shivers down her spine.

The winds still raged around them, whipping her cloak and tousling her hair, but the Duke's hold was unwavering. He had saved her from falling to her doom, and in doing so, he had become her savior, her protector.

As their eyes locked, she felt an inexplicable connection, an unspoken understanding that transcended the chaos of the storm. In that perilous moment on the edge of the cliff, she realized that the world could shift in the blink of an eye. Life was unpredictable, and sometimes, salvation arrived in the most unexpected form.

She wanted to express her gratitude, to thank him for his timely intervention, but words escaped her. Her heart raced, not just from the adrenaline of the near fall, but from the presence of the Duke, who held her as if he had known her for a lifetime. Every emotion, from the fear of the cliff's edge to the overwhelming relief of being saved, swirled within her.

In the midst of the storm and the tempestuous sea, Genevieve and the Duke stood together on the precipice of fate, their lives forever entwined by the thread of a perilous encounter and the unspoken connection that bound them.

Who was this man? What was so different about him?

Unlike the refined men she was familiar with, he possessed a certain rawness, a rugged quality that set him apart from the polished aristocrats of her world. His clothes were weathered, and his hands bore the calluses of hard work. Yet, it was his eyes that captured her interest. They conveyed a depth of emotion, a kindness that seemed at odds with his rough exterior, and to learn that he was the new duke had truly stunned her. Secretly, she had anticipated the Duke to be a much older gentleman, someone befitting the dignity of such a noble position.

But here he stood before her, young and undeniably handsome, just as Eleanor had predicted. His presence defied the image she had conjured in her mind. It was as though fate had played a whimsical trick on her, presenting a Duke who was both unexpected and captivating. What in the world was to transpire henceforth?

# CHAPTER 6

The wind cut sharply around Jonathan as he stood on the edge of the cliff, the biting cold making his skin tingle. But it was not the wind that held him captive; it was the sight of Lady Genevieve's rosy cheeks and the gratitude shining in her eyes. In that moment, her gaze seemed to pierce through the gust, and Jonathan could not help but be captivated by the warmth he found there.

Her presence was like a beacon, drawing him closer by the moment. Her slender figure, framed by a rich, beautiful gown, seemed to defy the raging winds. Her long, strawberry blonde tresses danced in the air, and her striking blue eyes held a depth that drew him in.

There was an ethereal quality about her, as if she were a creature of the sea herself, belonging to the cliffs and the waves. Her fair complexion was untouched by the wind's harshness, and it only accentuated the delicate beauty of her features.

As he continued to gaze at her, he was struck by a profound sense of wonder. In that fleeting moment, she appeared as a vision of grace and vulnerability, standing on the edge of the world. There was something about her, an allure that transcended the physical, and it left him captivated.

A noise, like the distant rumble of thunder, drew his attention away from Genevieve. He turned, his eyes widening as another figure emerged from the ruins. The unmistakable limp in the man's stride caught Jonathan's immediate attention. Concern surged within him, mingling with his curiosity.

"Genie?" the man asked curiously, with his head cocked to one side. "What is happening?"

Before Jonathan could jump to any conclusions or offer assistance, Genevieve took a step towards the man, her voice gentle but firm as she talked. "Your Grace, this is my brother, Lord Harry Ellsworth." Her words hung in the air, a surprising revelation that filled the moment with a blend of relief and intrigue.

Jonathan's gaze shifted between the siblings, and he could not help but marvel at the strange situation that had brought them together on the cliffs of Graftonshire.

"Lord Ellsworth." Jonathan smiled as he extended his hand to the new addition to their group. "It is wonderful to meet you."

"Lord Grantham is the new Duke of Graftonshire," Genevieve continued. "He just stopped me from having a terrible fall."

"Well, then I must thank you for caring for my sister," Harry laughed. "And it is lovely to meet you and to welcome you to Graftonshire. Are you enjoying living here?"

Jonathan paused thoughtfully for a moment, before he answered. "It may not be what I am used to, but it has a certain charm."

Although even as the words left his mouth, he was not sure if he meant the beautiful scenery from where he stood, or the captivating woman standing in front of him. Both caused his breath to get caught in his throat as he looked at them.

The three of them stood on the wind-swept cliffs, engaged in cordial conversation that bridged the gap between strangers. Jonathan found himself charmed by the candidness of Genevieve and the quiet strength that emanated from her brother, Harry. They were unlike anyone he had ever met before, and that intrigued him greatly.

Amidst the chat, the shifting weather did not escape Jonathan's notice. Impending storm clouds gathered on the horizon, darkening the sky and intensifying the howling winds. The weather seemed to mirror the uncertain path that lay before him, and Jonathan could not help but feel a sense of urgency in the air.

Harry's subtle cues were not lost on Jonathan either. The young man's eyes frequently flicked toward the darkening sky, and his body language conveyed an unspoken urgency to move from the open cliffs. It was as if he could sense the impending tempest and sought shelter from the approaching storm. Perhaps because of his limp, he was more attuned to these sorts of things.

"Perhaps we should make our way back home," Harry finally declared, voicing the concerns that had clearly been plaguing him for a little while. "The sky is darkening."

Jonathan did not miss the disappointment that crossed Genevieve's face. Was she enjoying the conversation as much as he was? He could almost still feel her resting in his arms, which was a sensation that he definitely enjoyed. He hoped that in time, their paths might cross again, perhaps at the ball his cousin and mother were throwing for him.

"Yes, I suppose so," Genevieve eventually agreed, before she bobbed down into a graceful curtsy. Jonathan had not spent a lot of time around refined women who behaved in this manner, so he felt a little awkward as he bowed back. "It was lovely to meet you, Your Grace."

He agreed, as did Harry, before it was time for them all to part. As he watched them recede in to the distance, their figures becoming smaller and more distant against the rugged backdrop of the landscape, a pang of something unnameable tugged at Jonathan's heart. It was a feeling that defied easy description, an emotion born of their chance encounter and the uncharted territory that had opened before him. Graftonshire was turning out to be a lot more exciting than he thought it would be.

With a mix of anticipation and uncertainty, Jonathan turned away from the cliffs and made his way back to the sanctuary of Grafton Estate. The impending storm was a metaphor for the unpredictable path that lay ahead, and he could not help but feel that the chapters of his life were becoming increasingly entwined with the enigmatic Lady Genevieve and her brother, Harry.

As Jonathan retraced his steps from the cliffs, an unshakable feeling of curiosity lingered within him, his thoughts lost on his new friends. But a sudden sight on the rocks nearby soon distracted him. He approached the spot with a sense of intrigue, his eyes narrowing as he examined the unknown object. There, half open and snagged on a rocky outcrop, lay a cloth bag. Its fabric bore a familiar color, one that immediately called to mind Genevieve's bonnet from earlier. That discovery left him both puzzled and concerned.

With a mixture of apprehension and curiosity, Jonathan reached for the small cloth bag. As he examined it more closely, he noticed that it was torn, as if it had been caught on the rocks during an attempt to secure it. It was a peculiar sight, and he could not help but wonder how it had ended up there. Did Genevieve lose more than her bonnet on the cliffs? She did not mention it, but perhaps there was no time to do so. Either that or she had not noticed.

Intrigued, he carefully opened the small bag and discovered two papers tucked inside. His heart quickened as he scanned his eyes over the elegant hand writing on one of the papers. It was a flowing script that hinted at an unsolved mystery and a hidden treasure within Graftonshire's boundaries.

But what captured his attention the most were the symbols and markings on the paper. They hinted at a map, a cryptic puzzle that seemed to hold the key to an extraordinary discovery. What was this? If this did belong to Genevieve then he needed to get it back to her, sooner rather than later.

\*\*\*

Later, ensconced in the quiet solitude of Graftonshire Manor's library, Jonathan found himself immersed in the world of historical records. The room was steeped in an atmosphere of antiquity, its shelves filled with volumes that held the secrets of generations past.

In his hands, he held an aged journal, its pages brittle and yellowed with time. The journal had been penned by his great uncle, a man of adventurous spirit and a love for exploration. As he turned the pages with care, the journal spoke of past adventures that had taken place within the very boundaries of Graftonshire.

The words on those time worn pages tantalizingly hinted at the existence of a hidden treasure, a mystery that had long eluded those who had sought it. The journal recounted stories of daring expeditions, cryptic clues, and encounters with ancient landmarks, all pointing towards a fabled prize buried within the heart of Graftonshire. All lead by the sort of map that Jonathan had found in that small cloth bag discovered at the cliff tops. Was this what Genevieve had been searching for when she was at the Seabrook Ruins? He had no idea, but it was terribly intriguing. In the short time he had spent with her, he had sensed an adventurous heart that mirrored his own.

Jonathan's heart quickened with a sense of anticipation as he delved deeper into the journal. He was now part of a legacy of explorers and adventurers who had been drawn to the allure of Graftonshire's hidden secrets. He had always had that spirit, he just did not know where to take it after his time on the ocean. But this might be just what he was looking for. The winds of change had brought him in to the fold, and he could not help but feel a profound connection to the history and mysteries that surrounded him.

Jonathan remained in the library for a very long time, engrossed in the pages of his great uncle's journal, the promise of hidden treasure lingering in his thoughts. The room was suffused with an air of history, and the anticipation of what lay ahead hung heavy in the air. He almost forgot that the rest of the world existed as he read on...

"Jonathan." That was until the sudden appearance of Lucas broke the spell that the journal had cast over him. Jonathan looked up, his mind still partially entrenched in the mysteries of Graftonshire's past. "What are you reading about?"

Jonathan leaned forward, his expression a mix of excitement and intrigue. "Lucas, you will not believe what happened today," he began, his voice carrying an undertone of excitement.

Lucas raised an eyebrow, his curiosity piqued. "Do tell, old friend. You seem positively charged with energy."

With a grin, Jonathan launched in to the tale of his fateful encounter on the cliffs, his voice animated as he described Lady Genevieve and her brother, Harry. He recounted how he had saved her bonnet and, in turn discovered the little bag. "It was incredible, Lucas. The entire affair resembled a passage from a splendid novel. And that, my dear friend, is not even the most captivating aspect," he added enigmatically.

Lucas leaned in closer, the fire light dancing in his eyes. "What could possibly be more fascinating than that, Jonathan?"

"Ah," Jonathan replied, taking a dramatic pause, "the map itself. You will not believe what I found inside the bag."

With an air of intrigue, he retrieved the small, folded paper from his pocket and placed it on the polished wooden desk between them. Lucas studied it intently, recognizing the symbols etched to the paper.

"Is this... a treasure map?" Lucas asked, his voice filled with curiosity.

Jonathan nodded. "A map that hints at a hidden treasure within Graftonshire itself."

Lucas's eyes widened, and he took a deep breath. "That sounds like something straight out of a legend."

Jonathan chuckled. "It does, I agree. But it gets even more interesting. I have been doing some research in the library. There is an aged journal written by my great uncle. It hints at past adventures and tantalizingly suggests the existence of a hidden treasure in Graftonshire. I believe it might be related to this very map."

Lucas leaned back in his chair, pondering the implications. "This is a remarkable turn of events, my friend. A hidden treasure and a map discovered within a little bag. It is almost too fantastic to be true. All on the same day that you meet Lady and Lord Ellsworth."

Jonathan's gaze was filled with excitement as he looked at Lucas. "I knew you would appreciate the mystery of it all, Lucas. There is something about Lady Genevieve and her brother, Lord Harry. It feels like the beginning of an extraordinary adventure."

As he spoke these words aloud, Jonathan realized that he *had* to follow this map, especially if Genevieve was doing the same thing. He was compelled to do so, to see what was next and what was hidden within his new home town.

# CHAPTER 7

The following day dawned with a sense of restlessness that enveloped Genevieve like a shroud. Her thoughts were consumed by the loss of her grandfather's letter and map, both of which had held the key to a treasure hidden within Graftonshire's boundaries. The sense of purpose and adventure that had ignited her spirit was now tainted by the weight of her missing documents. She could not believe that had happened, she had tried to be so careful with the map and the letter because they meant so much to her, but as she tripped and almost fell, she must have dropped them which put an end to her journey before she had even gotten a chance to find anything. She would never discover the hidden treasure now.

Unable to bear the uncertainty any longer, Genevieve felt an urgency to return to the cliffs, hoping against hope to retrieve what had been lost. She knew that her grandfather's words contained clues and riddles that were essential to unlocking the secrets of the hidden treasure, and she could not bear the thought of them falling into the wrong hands.

Turning to her younger brother who was sitting beside her in the drawing room, she expressed her concerns and the torment that gnawed at her heart. "Harry, I must go back to the cliffs," she said with a determination that was characteristic of her fiery spirit. "You know I have not been able to find our grandfather's map since we returned home, and I can only assume that I have left it behind there. I can not stand the idea of someone else finding it."

"You believe you lost it over the cliff?" Harry, whose affection for his sister ran deep, looked at her with a mixture of worry and understanding. He knew the depths of Genevieve's passion for adventure and her commitment to the quest they had unwittingly embarked upon. "Do you really think it can still be found this morning?"

Genevieve shook her head because she did not even want to consider that possibility. "I must try. I will never be able to forgive myself if I leave it behind. All the years that the treasure has been hidden, and I am the one who lost the map. I feel so horrible about it."

"Genevieve," Harry continued, his voice soft but laced with concern, "you must be cautious. The cliffs are perilous, and the elements can be unforgiving. Wandering there alone is dangerous, and I fear for your safety. I wish I could walk with you, but I am very tired today."

Genevieve knew what that meant. Harry would never specifically say that his leg was hurting because he did not want to upset her by reminding her of the accident. But that was where her mind instantly went. Guilt flowed through her, and she knew she could not ask Harry to join her once more. Could she go alone though? After what happened the day before, she was not sure. If it had not been for Harry and the duke, who knew what would have happened to her. It might have been herself lost, not the map and letter.

With a sigh, Harry continued, "But I have to admit, I am relieved that your recent encounter was with the Duke of Graftonshire. He seems to be a reputable and honorable individual who cared for you as you fell. It could have been far worse, Genevieve."

Genevieve nodded, acknowledging her brother's wisdom. "You are right, Harry. I must exercise caution and not let my impulsive nature lead me in to recklessness. I will take precautions... but I do want to return to the cliffs because I truly do wish to get the map back. I can not stop thinking about it."

Harry did not look happy about that, but thankfully he did not argue with her. "I understand. If you can wait a little, I will join you. I do not wish you to go alone."

"Ooh, are you talking about *him*?" All of a sudden, both Genevieve and Harry were stunned to see their cousin staring at them with a glimmer of delight in her eyes as she joined them. "Oh, Genevieve, you simply must share the details of your little encounter with the Duke. I can see it now — tantalizing secrets exchanged on the cliffs, a dash of mystery, and perhaps a stolen heart or two?" She playfully raised an eyebrow, hoping to infuse some light heartedness into the situation.

Genevieve, however, remained unwavering in her focus, her thoughts still consumed by the lost letter and map. She barely registered Eleanor's jests, her determination too strong to be swayed by playful banter. "Yes, he was very kind," she replied in a monotone voice. "But I am more concerned with going back to the cliffs so I can find what I lost."

But even as she said that, fate showed that it had other plans for her. The weather outside took a turn for the worse. Rain began to pour, a steady drumbeat against the window panes, further diminishing Genevieve's hopes of retrieving the precious documents.

Harry, ever the voice of reason, chimed in, "Given the rain, Genevieve, it is quite likely that the letter, if it had remained, would be ruined by now. The cliffs can be unsafe in this weather, and it is not worth the risk. Perhaps we can think of another way to decipher the clues in our grandfather's letter. A fresh perspective might lead us to the treasure. Perhaps we should return to the library and see if there are any more books with clues for us to work with."

Genevieve's shoulders slumped in reluctant agreement. The reality of the situation was beginning to sink in, and she knew that venturing out in such a storm would be reckless. But her determination burned as bright as ever, and she was determined to find another way to unravel the mysteries of Graftonshire's hidden treasure.

*** 

Later that afternoon, as the sun dipped below the horizon, casting a warm golden glow over Graftonshire Manor, Genevieve's bedchamber came alive with activity. Madeline, her loyal and skillful lady's maid, was meticulously arranging Genevieve's attire for the ball that was to take place that evening.

The gown, a creation of silk and lace, was a marvel of opulence and elegance. Its fabric shimmered in the soft, golden light of the chamber, and the intricate embroidery spoke of countless hours of dedicated craftsmanship. It was a garment that spoke of the grandeur and sophistication that was expected of the nobility in attendance at the ball.

The gown she had chosen for this momentous occasion was a vision of sheer luxury. It was an exquisite creation of ivory silk, its fabric so fine it felt like a whisper against her skin. The bodice was adorned with intricate lace, delicate as the morning dew, and embroidered with shimmering seed pearls that caught the light in a dazzling display. The gown's flowing skirt cascaded like a water fall, pooling around her feet in a cascade of fabric that seemed almost otherworldly.

The pièce de résistance was a sapphire pendant necklace, a family heirloom that had been passed down for generations. The brilliant blue gem, set in an ornate silver pendant, rested against the porcelain skin of her décolletage. Its elegance and history were not lost on Genevieve, and it served as a reminder of the legacy and responsibilities that weighed heavily on her shoulders.

As Madeline assisted Genevieve with her attire, her nimble fingers adjusted the fabric, ensuring every seam and fold lay perfectly. The gown was a stark contrast to the tumultuous emotions swirling within Genevieve. While she appeared every bit the elegant lady of the manor, her heart was a tempest of secrets, mysteries, and the ever elusive treasure that remained her ultimate quest.

Genevieve knew that this ball was more than just a social gathering; it was a stage for the intricate dance of society and a chance to gather information about the new duke, the man who had been on her mind as much as the map ever since she met him. But as Genevieve stood before the full length mirror, her reflection adorned in the resplendent gown, her appearance belied the turmoil that swirled within her. The glittering tiara resting atop her long, strawberry blonde tresses seemed to mock the storm of emotions she concealed.

Madeline, ever attentive to her mistress's needs, observed the unease that danced in Genevieve's eyes. She tightened the last of the corset laces and offered a comforting smile. "You look positively radiant, milady," Madeline said in her soft, reassuring tone. "I am sure tonight will be just as wonderful as you imagine."

Genevieve forced a smile in return, though it did little to ease the weight on her heart. The grand ball, a celebration of the Duke's recent ascension, was meant to be a night of joy and merriment. Yet, for Genevieve, it was but a brief interlude in the relentless pursuit of her family's secrets and the hidden treasure.

"Thank you, Madeline," she replied tautly. "I am sure it will be wonderful."

She had often heard it said that the aristocracy was skilled in masking their true emotions beneath a veneer of grace and composure, and Genevieve was determined to wear that mask with dignity tonight. As she descended the grand staircase, she knew that the night ahead would be filled with laughter, music, and dancing. But her thoughts would remain tethered to the mysteries that lay hidden within the heart of Graftonshire.

As the Ellsworth family arrived at the grand Graftonshire Manor for the evening's ball, the air was filled with a palpable sense of excitement and anticipation. The splendor of the estate, with its sprawling gardens and majestic façade, never failed to inspire awe, even in those who had visited many times before.

Genevieve's distress over the lost letter and map momentarily subsided as they were welcomed by Lady Agatha, who radiated warmth and grace. Her welcoming smile and gracious words were a balm to Genevieve's troubled heart, and she greeted the older lady with genuine affection. Lady Agatha's presence always brought a sense of comfort and familiarity to the grand estate.

However, as her gaze shifted past Lady Agatha while the lady talked to her parents, Genevieve's heart quickened its pace. There, standing beside his mother, was the Duke of Graftonshire himself, Jonathan Grantham. Their eyes met, and for a fleeting moment, time seemed to stand still. The vivid memories of their serendipitous meeting on the cliffs of Graftonshire rushed back to her, and the intensity of that encounter echoed in their locked gazes.

Their stare held a depth of connection that transcended the bounds of social propriety. It was as if the world around them faded into insignificance, leaving only the two of them, locked in a moment of shared understanding and unspoken emotions.

Eleanor, always astute to such matters, seized the opportunity to tease her older cousin. With a mischievous glint in her eye, she playfully chided Genevieve for her unladylike behavior in a whisper that thankfully no one else could hear. "Genevieve, I do believe you have forgotten your manners tonight," she said, her tone light and teasing. "Or perhaps you have simply lost yourself in the Duke's enigmatic, deep gaze?"

Genevieve blushed, her cheeks flushed with embarrassment. She was acutely aware of the impropriety of their lingering stare, and yet, it was as if a magnetic force had drawn her to Jonathan. The encounter on the cliffs had left an indelible mark on her, and now, in the heart of Graftonshire Manor, their paths had crossed once again. But Eleanor had reminded her that she needed to look away, whether she wanted to or not, causing an intense heat to race through her body. She knew she had probably started to shine red, which only made this much more humiliating. Thankfully, it was not long until it was time for Genevieve and her family to walk on.

As Genevieve and her family proceeded through the magnificent halls of Graftonshire Manor, Eleanor leaned in, her voice a playful whisper in Genevieve's ear, not quite finished with the teasing as yet. "My dear cousin, I must say the Duke of Graftonshire is quite striking, do you not think?" Her tone was light, and she wore a mischievous smile. "I wonder what it is like to talk to him. You will have to tell me more about your meeting with him because I am *very* intrigued by him..."

Genevieve's thoughts, however, were still caught in the whirlwind of emotions from her unexpected reunion with Jonathan. His presence, the vivid memory of their cliff-side encounter, and the intensity of their locked gazes continued to occupy her mind. She could not help but acknowledge the truth in Eleanor's words, though she made no reply.

Before she could gather her thoughts and respond to her cousin's teasing, an unsettling presence caught her attention. Across the grand ballroom, her eyes met those of Lord Alastair Fitzroy. The memories of the previous Season rushed back, particularly the awkward and painful instance when she had rejected his marriage proposal. The look of evident displeasure on Alastair's face was unmistakable, and a chill ran down Genevieve's spine.

The mere sight of Alastair, his eyes fixed on her, sent her stomach twisting into knots. She had known that her rejection had bruised his pride, but the intensity of his resentment was palpable. As they moved further into the ballroom, she could not shake the feeling that Alastair's presence would bring a storm of trouble to an otherwise enchanting evening.

It had been a beautiful evening, not unlike this one, when Alastair had taken her aside under the twinkling stars. In the soft glow of moon light, he had poured his heart out to her, his words laced with affection and longing. He had proposed to her with a genuine and earnest plea for her hand in marriage.

The memory of that night still made her shudder with embarrassment. She recalled the knot in her stomach as she struggled to find the right words, the weight of the eyes of the assembled guests upon her. She had turned him down, gently but firmly, explaining that her feelings for him did not match his own, and that she could not accept his proposal. The look of disappointment and humiliation on Alastair's face had been etched into her memory, and it had cast a shadow over her in subsequent social gatherings.

As Genevieve relived that moment in her mind, she could not help but wonder if Alastair's presence at the ball would bring with it a resurgence of those uncomfortable feelings and strained interactions. The memory of her rejection still weighed heavily on her heart, and she knew that facing Alastair once more would not be an easy task.

# CHAPTER 8

Lord Alastair Fitzroy, a tall and well dressed figure, stood regally beside his cousin, the Duchess of Cavendale, in the grand ballroom of Graftonshire Manor. The chandeliers over head cast a warm, golden glow upon the gathering, and the ornate room was filled with aristocrats in their finest attire. By his side were the Duchess's husband, the Duke of Cavendale, and their young daughter, Lady Isabella. They had come to spend the winter season in Graftonshire and were eagerly participating in the social festivities.

Alastair's attention, however, was undeniably fixed on someone else.

Lady Genevieve Ellsworth, with her strawberry blonde curls cascading gracefully down her back, had captured his interest from the moment she entered the ballroom. She was the undeniable star of the evening, her presence radiant, and her graceful demeanor leaving a trail of admirers in her wake. Her slender figure, enhanced by a beautifully crafted gown, was a vision of elegance and poise.

But unbeknownst to Lady Genevieve, Alastair did not count himself as one of her admirers, although he could not take his eyes off of her. He observed her movements, the delicate curve of her smile, and the charm that flowed from her like a beacon in the night. Amid the lively conversations and the enchanting waltz music that filled the room, Alastair found himself solely focused on Lady Genevieve. Her presence transported him to the previous year, when he had been a darling of society, an eligible bachelor sought after by ambitious families, and Genevieve's considerable dowry had been the key that unlocked his ambitions.

Alastair's thoughts drifted back to the days when his pursuit of Lady Genevieve was not driven by true love but by a desperate ploy to secure her wealth and stave off the impending bankruptcy that threatened his social status. It was a time when he was a master of deception, a charmer of hearts, and a collector of fortunes… or so he thought. So he hoped.

He had been a brilliant actor, skillfully playing the part of the ardent suitor. In the eyes of the world, he was the perfect match for Lady Genevieve. He had whispered sweet promises and spun a web of romance that had lured her in. At the time, it had seemed so easy, so natural to manipulate her emotions.

But Alistair had never considered the possibility that Genevieve might possess an independent spirit, a fierce determination, and a heart that could not be easily won by his artful words. He had underestimated her, believing that her wealth was her most valuable asset, the one he needed to secure. He thought that she would easily go along with whatever her parents wanted, and that she would not be given a choice of her own.

But she most certainly did have a mind of her own, and that was Alistair's down fall.

The chilling memory of her rejection remained etched in his mind. Her refusal had been a stark reminder that Lady Genevieve Ellsworth was not a pawn to be won in his game of social survival. She had seemingly seen through his facade, recognized his ulterior motives, and dared to defy his advances.

Either that, or she simply did not want him.

No matter what, the bitterness of that rejection had haunted him ever since. It was a harsh lesson in humility, one that had tarnished his reputation and, in many ways, destroyed his standing within the elite circles of society. No one seemed to look at him in the same way anymore, which Alistair hated.

Alistair watched Lady Genevieve with a mixture of anger and intense regret that he had not managed to make things work out with her. Her grace, her beauty, and the strength she had displayed by standing up to him had remained etched in his memory, making the loss of her dowry that much harder to bear.

As Alistair Fitzroy watched Lady Genevieve from across the grand ballroom, he could feel the bitterness swelling within him. The opulent surroundings, the lively chatter of the aristocracy, and the grandeur of Graftonshire Manor all seemed to blur into a meaningless backdrop. It was a stark contrast to the turmoil that raged within him.

His current financial predicament was all too real, and so much worse than it was the previous year when she could have saved him, and it was the gnawing anxiety of teetering on the brink of bankruptcy that had brought him to Graftonshire. Alistair Fitzroy, once the darling of high society, had fallen from grace, hard, and his once impeccable reputation now hung by the thinnest thread. His extravagant lifestyle, reckless investments, and gambling debts had left him in financial ruins.

He had been a master of disguises and had masked his troubles well, putting on a facade of prosperity that fooled many. But behind closed doors, the debtors had grown relentless, and the bailiffs had become all too familiar. The grandeur and luxury he had once enjoyed had turned into a mirage, and the weight of his financial burden had crushed his pride. The only person that Alistair could think to blame for that was Lady Genevieve. Things could have been resolved if only she had married him, if only he had received the dowry. If he could have used that money to get himself back on track, then he would still be revered by other people, not looked down on.

Alistair felt like even his family looked down on him these days. His cousin might have been beside him, but he did not feel even a scrap of support from her. She was merely there in the room beside him. No wonder he was so full of rage for Lady Genevieve. He wished that she could know what she had done to him, how she ruined his life. Especially since she did not look like she was suffering over everything that happened last year.

As bitterness coursed through him, threatening to consume him whole, Alistair's thoughts were interrupted by the sight of another figure in the room. Lord Jonathan Grantham, the newly appointed Duke of Graftonshire, had captured his attention. The man who everyone was here to celebrate. A man that Alistair did not realize he knew before this very moment...

But now as he stared at this man, it hit Alistair that their paths had not merely crossed in ballrooms or society gatherings before now; they had once shared a ship, a voyage, and a heart wrenching tragedy at sea. The memories of those fateful days came rushing back to Alistair, almost drowning him in the pain from the past.

Alistair had never sailed with Jonathan Grantham before the day of the tragedy, but he had heard good things about him. He did not think twice about the journey, especially because of his best friend, Trevor, had nothing but good things to say about the man.

How Alistair wished that he could go back in time to stop himself and Trevor from getting on that ship.

The memories of that ill fated voyage continued to haunt Alistair, even to this day. He could still hear the cries of their fellow sailors, feel the relentless fury of the tempest, and remember the desperate moments when their ship had been on the brink of destruction. Jonathan was supposed to be a beacon of leadership during those tumultuous times, a steady hand that had guided the crew through the darkest hours. But that was not how Alistair had felt. Especially as Trevor was tossed overboard in the storm that they *never* should have been sailing in, and he was never seen again. Alistair might not have actively seen him drown, but he knew that was what had happened.

Jonathan killed Trevor, and had also ruined Alistair's life. He was another person who Alistair could blame for everything.

As Alistair's eyes locked on to Jonathan from across the grand ballroom, all the emotions hit him hard. His hands curled up in to fists by his side and he was not sure how on earth he would be able to contain himself. How had this man gone from murdering his friend and other sailors that day, to Duke of Graftonshire? It did not seem fair.

Alistair forced himself to turn away from this man from his past so he could gather himself up. Much as he wanted to let Jonathan know how much damage he had caused, Alistair knew that fighting in the middle of the ballroom would not help his reputation. He certainly could not make things worse for himself.

Alistair's contemplation of the past was abruptly interrupted as the host of the evening, Lady Agatha Grantham, resplendent in her grandeur, approached him. She was accompanied by none other than the newly appointed Duke of Graftonshire, Jonathan Grantham himself, and another very elegant woman beside him. The trio approached Alistair with a grace and formality that was characteristic of the highest echelons of society.

"Lord Fitzroy," Lady Agatha greeted him with a warm smile. "May I present to you the Duke of Graftonshire, Jonathan Grantham, and his mother, Lady Rosalind Grantham."

Alistair, though disoriented by the sudden shift in focus, managed a polite and well practiced smile. He bowed his head ever so slightly in acknowledgment. "Your Grace, Lady Rosalind," he said with a slight nod, his tone a fine blend of cordiality and respect.

Jonathan returned the polite remoteness, as if he held no guilt over what happened to Trevor and the other men aboard the ship. "Lord Fitzroy, it is a pleasure to make your acquaintance."

As Alistair observed the trio while they exchanged pleasantries, he could not help but feel a sense of iciness trickling down his spine. He could not help but fixate on the face of the new Duke of Graftonshire. Their eyes finally met properly, but much to Alistair's surprise, the connection was devoid of any warmth, any hint of recognition. Instead, Jonathan's gaze bore indifference, as if their paths had never crossed, as if their shared history and tragedy held no significance.

The absence of recognition, the sheer lack of acknowledgment, left Alistair bewildered and irate. How could the Duke forget? How could he dismiss the tumultuous voyage they had once shared, the perils they had faced together, and the lives that had been lost at sea? Or was this indifference a deliberate act, an intentional over sight meant to erase their shared past from the annals of his memory? Whatever it was, it made Alistair incredibly unhappy and even more full of rage than he was before.

As the grand ball commenced and couples glided gracefully on to the dance floor, Alistair's thoughts took a decisive turn. The opulent ballroom, resplendent with the gleam of jewels and the hushed rustle of expensive fabric, presented more than an evening of social amusement. It held within its adorned walls an opportunity — a chance to secure his future by pursuing a lady of consequence, ideally one with a substantial dowry, to alleviate the financial burdens weighing heavily on his once proud lineage. One that would not refuse him.

Time was a relentless adversary, and the specter of impending bankruptcy loomed ever larger. With each passing day, his options dwindled, and his desperation swelled. The ballroom, this hub of affluence and potential alliances, was a battlefield where fortunes were decided as swiftly as the next waltz.

Surveying the room, Alistair contemplated the eligible ladies who graced the occasion. Some were heiresses, others daughters of influential families. As he watched them twirl with their dance partners, he assessed their prospects and pondered the implications of forging a connection with one of them.

His need for a solution was acute. The Fitzroy name, once revered and esteemed, had been tarnished by the inexorable march of debt. And he, the last male heir, bore the weight of that legacy's decay. The ballroom was, at this very moment, a theater of hope and strategy, where alliances could be forged, and futures could be reshaped.

With his course of action clear, Alistair ventured further into the glittering ballroom, ready to dance the dance of opportunity and secure his family's place in the upper echelons of society once more.

# CHAPTER 9

Jonathan's steps gracefully matched the rhythm of the waltz as he twirled across the grand ballroom with Lady Isabella, the Duchess of Cavendale's daughter. Her eyes sparkled with vivaciousness, and she leaned in closer, her gestures laden with subtle innuendos. Isabella had a reputation for her beauty and her aspirations to climb the social ladder. Jonathan was well aware that his newly acquired title as the Duke of Graftonshire made him an attractive prospect for many women, including Lady Isabella.

Despite her charms, Jonathan's thoughts wandered, hijacked by the unexpected encounter with Lord Alastair Fitzroy earlier in the evening. There was no denying that was strange, and Alastair's presence had stirred memories and suspicions, yet Jonathan could not pin point the precise connection that tied them together. The past held a shadowy figure who had once crossed his path in a tale etched in the ink of adversity. If only he could recall where he once knew that face. It might help him understand why Lord Fitzroy looked at him with disdain.

Yet for now, he could not focus on that unusual interaction. The lady in front of him demanded his attention.

As Isabella's laughter tinkled and her hand inched closer to his arm, Jonathan's tried to focus, but it was hard to stop his gaze from wandering around the room. The elaborate chandeliers cast a shimmering radiance across the room, bathing the opulent ballroom in a warm glow. Couples glided in harmonious cadence, lost in the beauty of the dance, while the whispered melodies of violins lent a soothing backdrop to the evening.

As the final notes of the waltz concluded, Jonathan led Lady Isabella back to the edge of the dance floor and executed a courteous bow. The gleam of the grand ballroom surrounded them, aglow with the grace and charm of society's finest.

"It was wonderful to dance with you," Isabella smiled coyly with a light blush filling her cheeks. "If you would ever like to dance again…"

There was a definite suggestion there that she wanted to dance with him a lot more, which would lead to the idea that he was courting her. Rumors and gossip would fly, and once the ton started to talk about marriage prospects, it was not easy to escape the expectations that would come with it. Jonathan was *not* a man who would fall in love and get married, even if he had taken on a Dukedom now. He needed to create a distance between Lady Isabella and himself before she pushed this further.

"Please, enjoy the rest of the evening," he declared with a polite bow instead. "Thank you."

As he turned away from Isabella, he caught sight of Lord Fitzroy across the other side of the ballroom, again causing a nagging feeling in the back of his head. There was definitely a memory there, but for now he still could not find it. Perhaps someone else, a friend, would be able to assist him in recalling this memory.

His path naturally led him to the refreshment table, where Captain Lucas Beaumont stood, cradling a crystal goblet of champagne. Their moment of silence as they stood beside one another spoke volumes, carrying with it the weight of shared history, loyalty, and unwavering trust. Jonathan knew that he wanted to ask about Lord Alistair Fitzroy, but he just needed a little moment of peace before he brought up the strange figure from his past.

But before he got the chance to say a word, Jonathan noticed someone else headed towards him. Lord Harry Ellsworth. Now what could Genevieve's brother want with him? They had only met one another once, at the cliff top, so he could only assume that their conversation would be about that.

"Your Grace," Harry began, a hint of unease in his voice as he finally got close enough for Jonathan to hear him, "I wanted to... to express my gratitude. I am truly thankful you were there on the cliffs to prevent my sister from having a terrible fall."

Jonathan could not stop the giant smile from spreading across his face as they talked about Genevieve. He could still very starkly recall the sensation of Genevieve in his arms as he stopped her from tumbling. There was an excitement that immediately brewed between them, that only the two of them could understand.

He nodded in acknowledgment, a subtle but sincere gesture of acceptance. "I understand, Lord Ellsworth. I am glad that I could be of assistance. There is no need for apologies. I do very much appreciate you coming to speak with me though. I am happy to talk to you any time."

"That is terribly kind of you. It is wonderful to get acquainted with the new Duke of Graftonshire."

As Harry smiled, offering a gracious nod and a slight bow before he turned to leave, Jonathan could not help but notice the limp in his step once again. It was a pronounced and heavy limp that hinted at an injury, one that must have been both painful and serious.

Watching Harry depart, Jonathan's chest tightened with a mixture of concern and curiosity. It was evident that something significant had occurred to cause such a noticeable injury. His mind raced with possible scenarios, imagining the circumstances that might have led to such a condition. It must have been something terrible, he thought, and he wondered if Harry carried the emotional scars of that event as well.

Deep inside, Jonathan knew he would never ask Harry about the nature of the injury or the events that had led to it. Such inquiries would be invasive and insensitive, and Harry's privacy deserved to be respected. However, his curiosity remained, a silent undercurrent that tugged at his thoughts, leaving him to wonder about the untold stories that lay behind the limping figure of Genevieve's brother. "Who is that?" Lucas asked, intrigued as he edged closer to his side.

"He is Lord Harry Ellsworth. I met him and his sister by the Seabrook Ruins. I believe that they are my neighbours."

"I see. Is his sister here too?"

Jonathan's eyes scanned the grand ballroom, filled with elegant guests, shimmering gowns, and dashing gentlemen. And then, as if drawn by an invisible force, his gaze landed on Genevieve, resplendent in her ivory gown that seemed to cascade around her like a waterfall of moon light. She stood on the edge of the dance floor, a vision of grace and elegance.

It was a surprising sight to see her there, on the periphery of the dance. Jonathan could not help but wonder how she had found a spare moment amidst the swirl of the evening's festivities. Genevieve's presence was like a beacon, casting a glow that was impossible to ignore.

He marveled at how every gentleman in the room had to be longing for a dance with her. Her beauty was undeniable, but it was her warmth and intelligence that set her apart.

"There she is," he half whispered as he pointed her out. "Lady Genevieve Ellsworth."

"I see," Lucas replied with a sly smile playing on his lips. "She is a very beautiful woman. It must have been lovely to meet her. I am sure you were captivated."

Jonathan could hear the teasing in his friend's tone, and he could not handle that tonight, so he knew that it was time for him to start the rounds, to make sure that all of his guests felt welcome. He shot Lucas a playful warning look before he walked off. He navigated through the vibrant crowd, a cordial smile gracing his face as he exchanged pleasantries with various guests. He was a Duke now, and it was his duty to engage with the assembled company, whether he wanted to or not. This could not have been further from life at sea if it tried, but Jonathan was doing his best to make the best of his new life, however hard it was.

Then, amidst the sea of familiar and unfamiliar faces, Lady Agatha appeared, bringing Lady Genevieve and her father, Mr. Ellsworth, in to his path. Their conversation flowed effortlessly, a dance of words and smiles that hinted at the enchantment of the evening. They spoke of trivial matters, the weather, and the beauty of the ballroom, but beneath the surface, there was an unspoken connection between Genevieve and himself, a silent understanding that seemed to bridge the gap between their worlds.

Genevieve's beauty was undeniable, her features a delicate combination of grace and elegance. But it was the air of quiet confidence that surrounded her that left a lasting impression on Jonathan. Her poise and the way she carried herself in the midst of the opulent soirée were captivating.

In the background, the waltz began, its melodic strains filling the room with an enchanting rhythm. As the music swirled around them, Jonathan felt an inexplicable internal nudge urging him to seize the moment. He knew, even before he asked, that he wanted to share this dance with Lady Genevieve.

With a slight smile, he extended his hand to her. "Lady Genevieve, would you do me the honour of this dance?"

Her response was swift and affirmative, as she placed her hand in his. "I would be delighted, Your Grace."

As they moved on to the dance floor, the world around them seemed to melt away. The sensation of her gloved hand in his sent an unexpected thrill coursing through him, a surge of electricity that caught him entirely off guard. He had danced with many women before, but this was different — this was Lady Genevieve. The elegance of the waltz, combined with Lady Genevieve's ethereal presence, created an atmosphere of enchantment. They glided gracefully, step in sync with step, Jonathan's hand at the small of her back, and hers resting gently on his shoulder. The grand ballroom faded into the background, and for those fleeting moments, it was as if they were the only two people in the world which was a wonderful sensation, unlike anything that Jonathan had ever felt before. It would have been very easy for him to get captivated by this feeling, to get swept away by it, but of course he knew that could not happen. He would never truly let anyone in to his heart again, not after what had happened in the past. He could not, he would not.

For Jonathan, the dance felt like the weaving of destiny, a reminder that life had a way of bringing people together when the time was right. Their synchronized movements spoke of a harmony that extended beyond the physical. Lady Genevieve's presence was captivating, and it felt as though they were connected on a deeper level. He noticed the way her blue eyes sparkled with life, the grace with which she moved, and the subtle hints of a smile playing on her lips.

He could not help but wonder about the future, about the uncharted territory that seemed to stretch out before them. Yet, amidst this enchantment, a burning question simmered within him. The memory of seeing her on the cliffs could not be ignored. It tugged at the back of his mind, insisting on being addressed.

As they twirled gracefully across the floor, their steps so in tune that it felt like a shared reverie, Jonathan found the courage to speak. "Lady Genevieve," he began, his voice low, "I could not help but wonder about the encounter on the cliffs. What brought you to such a perilous place in such terrible weather?"

Their eyes met, and he noticed a hint of surprise in her gaze. For a moment, he saw something deeper, a fleeting vulnerability beneath her composed exterior. He sensed that there were secrets she was holding back, stories that remained untold. Her response might hold the key to the enigma that was Lady Genevieve, and Jonathan was determined to unravel it. He could only hope that she would be open to letting him in enough to find everything out about her.

# CHAPTER 10

As Genevieve gracefully flowed with Jonathan across the dance floor, each step felt like a question and answer between them. The ballroom's elegant ambiance, bathed in soft candle light, was the perfect setting for this dance. The music, a slow and haunting melody, seemed to mirror the emotions that swirled within her. Their movements were seamless, as if they had danced together countless times before. She could not help but marvel at how well they complemented each other, how their bodies seemed to anticipate each other's every move. It was as if they were in perfect sync, two souls intertwined in a delicate and intricate dance. Genevieve had no idea what that meant, but she was enjoying the sensation nonetheless.

But within her, emotions swirled like a tempest. The dance was a beautiful facade, a delicate masquerade that hid the complex feelings she harbored. Her heart raced, and her breath quickened with every step. There was a magnetic pull between them, a connection that transcended the graceful motions of the dance.

Jonathan's eyes, intense and inviting, seemed to hold a thousand unspoken words. In their shared movements, she found herself asking questions without words and receiving answers in the subtle shifts of his body. It was a silent conversation that spoke volumes, a dance that went beyond the physical.

As they twirled and swayed, the emotions within her intensified. It was a blend of longing and uncertainty, a sense of being drawn into a world of unknown possibilities. She could not deny the pull she felt toward Jonathan, the way he made her pulse race and her thoughts whirl at the speed of light. But amidst the beauty of the dance, there was also a tangle of questions, doubts, and fears. She could not seem to shake off her worries however hard she tried.

Thoughts of her recent escapades at the cliffs kept surfacing in Genevieve's mind as she found herself drawn in to the intense gaze of Jonathan. Their shared moments upon the cliff top had created a connection between them, yet there were secrets she kept locked away. How might he react if he knew of her clandestine searches, she wondered. No one else seemed too pleased about her quest to find the treasure, even Harry who had helped her out as much as he could, so it was unlikely that Jonathan would take the news well either...

Not that it mattered, since she could no longer continue on with the quest. The library did not have any other information about the treasure, so it seemed like she had come to a dead end. The vexing loss of her grandfather's letter and map weighed heavily on her. The precious heirlooms that had led her to the cliffs were now gone, disappeared in the midst of her investigations. She longed to find them again, not just for her own sake but for the legacy they held. It was a burden she carried in silence, one that had taken a toll on her sleepless nights and restless days. But what if her brother was right, and the documents were going to be far too ruined now to ever read them?

"Lady Genevieve," Jonathan spoke in a soft, kind hearted tone of voice, shaking Genevieve from her thoughts "I could not help but wonder about the encounter on the cliffs. What brought you to such a perilous place in such terrible weather?"

Jonathan's inquiry was not invasive, but it was laced with genuine curiosity, which made her want to give him an answer of some kind. But she was not sure how honest she could be. Genevieve felt a rush of emotions at the question. Still, she decided to tread carefully, her response guarded. "I have some cherished memories associated with the cliffs," she replied, her voice holding a touch of wistfulness. "It is a place where I find solace and reflection. Sometimes, I go there to remember."

The dance continued, and amidst the graceful movements, there was a brief moment of respite. It was during this pause in their elegant twirls that Jonathan subtly indicated something, a folded paper he was safeguarding. Her heart raced as she recognized the familiar creases and edges of the map. It was her map, the very map she had believed to be lost forever, along with the cryptic letter from her grandfather. The folded paper held her family's history, and as she caught a glimpse of it, a rush of emotions surged through her. Surprise and disbelief mixed with an overwhelming sense of relief. It was a moment of revelation she hadn't anticipated. How had he come across these cherished artifacts?

Jonathan's voice broke through her racing thoughts. "Lady Genevieve," he said, his tone holding a mix of amusement and excitement, "I stumbled upon these at the Seabrook Ruins after Harry and you had departed. I thought you might be looking for them. I have kept them safe for you."

She was at a loss for words, struggling to understand the implications of his words. Her map and the letter, long thought to be lost, were now in Jonathan's possession. It was a revelation that filled her with intrigue, leaving her with a burning curiosity about how he had come across them.

Jonathan's gaze met hers, and he continued, his voice taking on a playful note. "Perhaps we could join forces in our quest for hidden treasures. Two heads are better than one, and our shared adventures have already proven to be quite extraordinary. Plus, I do not think it is a good idea for you to visit the cliff tops alone. We would not want you to fall without me there to catch you."

His admission and his suggestion hung in the air, and she could not help but smile. It was an offer she would never have expected, and it filled her with a mixture of surprise, relief, and intrigue. The possibility of a joint treasure quest with Jonathan was an idea that held immense promise and excitement. She did not give him an answer, but she offered him a sweet smile that let him know she was not opposed to the idea. He had truly surprised her by being the first person to be extremely positive about the quest.

"I am truly grateful that you found the documents and kept them safe for me." She grinned. "I do not like to think what would have happened if you had not discovered it. It might have been lost to the water forever. Then I would never know what my grandfather wanted me to search for."

As they resumed their dance, the echoes of his revelation lingered in her mind. The unspoken promise of what lay ahead, the shared quests and uncharted territories they could explore together, added a new layer of depth to their growing connection. The dance floor became a stage for a new chapter in their adventure, one that held the potential for untold discoveries and the unraveling of long held secrets.

As the dance continued, Genevieve felt the weight of it in a new way. It was not just the physical motion and the rhythm of their steps but the dance of understanding and mutual discovery between Jonathan and her. The music, their conversation, and the shared secrets all converged to create a sense of something larger, something that pointed towards an unfolding adventure.

With every step, she could sense the unspoken promise of their journey ahead. The dance, both literal and metaphorical, was a reflection of their growing connection. It was a dance of shared experiences, a dance of trust and vulnerability, and most importantly, a dance of understanding.

Jonathan's revelation about finding her lost map and the cryptic letter was a turning point. It was a symbol of their shared commitment to their quest for hidden treasures and the uncharted territories of their own hearts. Their conversations had become a silent exchange of questions and answers, of shared dreams and aspirations.

The music played on, its melody echoing in her heart. The dance had become more than just an elegant duet; it was now a reflection of the adventure they were embarking on. It was a symbol of their shared purpose, of the secrets they had uncovered, and the journey they were ready to undertake.

The weight of the dance was no longer a burden but a privilege. It was a celebration of the connection they were building, a testament to the shared dreams and the unspoken promises that bound them together. As they twirled and glided across the floor, Genevieve couldn't help but feel a profound sense of excitement and anticipation. The unfolding adventure, both in search of hidden treasures and the deepening connection between them, was a path she was eager to follow. Perhaps she would not have to do this on her own anymore. Maybe the duke was serious when he offered his assistance which would be really great for her.

As the waltz continued to carry Genevieve and Jonathan across the grand ballroom floor, she could not help but let her thoughts drift in to the realm of imagination. The conversation about embarking on a quest for hidden treasures with Jonathan had sparked a vibrant day dream, and she could not resist envisioning what it would be like to go on such an adventure with him. The enigmatic duke who had rescued her at the cliff tops.

In her mind's eye, she saw them as the protagonists of an exciting novel, their quest akin to the plot of a thrilling and mysterious tale. They would journey through ancient forests, explore hidden caves, and decipher cryptic clues. The wind would whisper secrets, and the stars would guide their way as they pursued the elusive treasures of Graftonshire.

The prospect of uncovering long forgotten histories and untold riches filled her with a sense of wonder and excitement. It was as if the stories of her childhood, filled with tales of hidden treasures and daring explorers, were coming to life before her very eyes. And to have such a wonderful gentleman on her arm would be a whole lot of fun.

The waltz became a dance of dreams, a dance where reality and imagination intertwined. As they moved in perfect harmony to the music, her heart brimmed with the possibilities of the adventures they could share, the stories they could create, and the mysteries they could unravel together.

Genevieve wondered if Jonathan's thoughts were mirroring her own, if he too was lost in the tantalizing day dreams of their potential future shared adventures. The glint of mischief dancing in his eyes as they continued to waltz suggested that he might be just as captivated by the possibilities as she was.

As they moved gracefully across the dance floor, she stole a glance at him. His gaze met hers, and the spark of playful anticipation was unmistakable. It was as if their connection had allowed them to share not only words but also unspoken dreams.

The thought that Jonathan might be imagining the same thrilling quests and hidden treasures, that he might see their journey as the plot of an extraordinary novel, added a layer of intimacy to their growing connection. It was a silent understanding that transcended words, a connection that hinted at the promise of shared adventures.

The dance, with its graceful movements and the melodic strains of the music, became a canvas for their mutual imagination. It was a dance of shared dreams and unspoken promises, a dance that deepened the bond between them.

As they twirled and swayed, Genevieve could not help but feel that they were both authors of the tale they were living, crafting a story that held the allure of hidden treasures, the thrill of uncharted territories, and the warmth of their growing connection. It was a dance of dreams, and in that moment, it felt as though they were sharing not just a waltz but the pages of an unwritten novel. How delightful and diverting!

# CHAPTER 11

Following the final note of the waltz, tradition dictated that the guests escorted their dance partners to the supper room. The evening had been filled with elegant movements, shared secrets, and unspoken promises, and now, as Jonathan linked his arm with Genevieve's, the subtle scent of lavender enveloped him, making everything feel so much more exciting. It was a scent that he was sure he would associate with her forever more.

As Jonathan walked alongside Genevieve, leading her to the supper room, he found himself utterly entranced by her presence. The elegance of the evening, the soft glow of candle light, and the enchanting atmosphere of the ballroom seemed to pale in comparison to her radiance. It was as if a spell had been cast, leaving him momentarily speechless.

Her beauty, grace, and poise had a captivating quality that left him mesmerized. He had never experienced such a magnetic pull before, a force that made it difficult for him to find his words. In her presence, the world seemed to fade into the background, and all that existed was the captivating figure at his side.

He was aware of every delicate movement, the way her gown seemed to flow with each step, and the subtle scent of lavender that enveloped her. The silence between them was not an awkward one but a shared appreciation of the moment, a recognition of the extraordinary connection they were building.

As they entered the supper room, Jonathan could not help but marvel at the depth of his feelings. He had been to countless gatherings and balls, but none had left him so entranced. In Genevieve, he had found something extraordinary, a connection that defied explanation and left him yearning for more.

The dance and the evening had brought them together, and now, as they shared the intimate setting of the supper room, he could not help but wonder what the future held for them. The enchantment of the night seemed to whisper promises of shared adventures, secrets, and a connection that was unlike any he had ever known. He did not usually trust his heart and where it was leading him, but in this moment, he could not help but follow along because he liked where he was going.

The moment Jonathan and Genevieve stepped in to the supper room, he was met with a scene of enchanting elegance. The room exuded an atmosphere of intimacy and refinement, illuminated by the soft, golden glow of countless candles that adorned the tables and walls. The flickering flames cast dancing shadows that seemed to add an extra layer of enchantment to the setting. His cousin had organized a wonderful night to celebrate him, and he truly was grateful to Lady Agatha for that.

The long, polished mahogany table was elegantly set with fine china, crystal glass ware, and gleaming silver ware. Delicate white linens draped the table, and floral arrangements of roses and lilies added a touch of natural beauty to the opulent surroundings. The room was filled with the low hum of conversation and the clinking of utensils against china, creating a harmonious background to the shared moments of the evening.

As they took their seats at the table, Jonathan could not help but appreciate the attention to detail in the room's design. The intricate wood work and the ornate chandeliers that hung from the ceiling were a testament to the grandeur of the mansion. It was a setting that perfectly matched the grandness of the evening and the enchantment that seemed to surround Genevieve.

The supper room, with its rich decor and the anticipation of the meal to come, was a place where shared secrets and conversations would continue to unfold. As Jonathan and Genevieve settled into their seats, the room held the promise of a new chapter in their adventure, where the mysteries of the past and the uncharted territories of the future would be explored over a sumptuous meal.

Amidst the enchanting atmosphere of the beautiful supper room, Jonathan's attention was briefly diverted by a sight that caught the corner of his eye. A fleeting look of disappointment, so unexpected, momentarily captured his attention. It was Isabella, a woman known for her unwavering composure, who sent a pointed glance in his direction.

Isabella's usually composed demeanor had faltered, and the emotions behind her gaze seemed to break through the carefully maintained facade she typically wore. Her disappointment, perhaps tinged with a hint of jealousy, was a revelation that left

Jonathan somewhat bewildered. He certainly was not expecting that.

He could have very easily gotten caught up in that look from Lady Isabella, and what the stare meant, if it were not for the captivating woman beside him. It was only a moment before his attention was drawn back to Lady Genevieve, and everything else was forgotten.

Amidst the lively chatter and the melodious clinking of glasses, Jonathan's thoughts became consumed by the old journal he had unearthed in his library. Its tales of turbulent seas, treasures hidden deep within the heart of Graftonshire, and the enigmatic hints about Grafton Moors holding a pivotal clue seemed to play on an endless loop in his mind.

The secrets and stories contained within the pages of the journal had taken root in his thoughts, like ivy vines slowly creeping into every corner of his consciousness. The journal had become a source of intrigue, a portal to a world of hidden treasures and untold adventures.

It made the map and Genevieve's grandfather's letter weight even heavier in Jonathan's pocket, a constant reminder of the cross roads he now faced. It was a dilemma that tugged at his conscience, and he could not help but feel the weight of the choice that loomed before him: to ensnare Genevieve in this unfolding enigma or to keep her safely distant from the mysteries that could change the course of their lives.

Not that it was only his choice of course. Genevieve was a strong willed woman, who would likely do whatever she wanted, no matter what advice he gave her. But that only drew him to her more. That made her even more intriguing to him.

Perhaps it would be easier if he let her know how much he understood her intrigue.

"You know, I found a journal in my family library," he said quietly to Genevieve, making sure that no one else overheard her. "One that belonged to my Great Uncle."

"You did?" Genevieve's eyes lit up in the way he hoped they would. "Pray, enlighten me further."

"The journal," he said, his voice low and filled with mystery, "it speaks of ancient legends and hidden treasures buried deep within the moors of Graftonshire. Tales of brave adventurers and elusive clues that could unlock the secrets of the past. It is a legacy that's been passed down through generations, a story of intrigue and wonder. Does that remind you of anything? Because it certainly reminds me of the items I found, the ones you lost at the Seabrook Ruins."

"Oh my!" Genevieve clapped her hands to her mouth in shock. "That is more evidence that there truly is something to be found."

From the inner pocket of his suit, Jonathan produced the map and letter and finally presented them to Genevieve. Her eyes widened with joy as she realized what he was offering. Her smile, radiant and filled with gratitude, sent his heart racing in response. It was a silent exchange, a clandestine connection between two souls who had been drawn together by fate and intrigue. She now had her belongings back, but hopefully she felt much less alone with these secrets because he understood her intrigue and he knew why she needed to find the treasure. He truly did hope that Genevieve would allow him to help her on her journey.

"Thank you, ever so much, Your Grace. This means the world to me."

"Please," he replied. "Call me Jonathan."

Her smile, warm and captivating, sent Jonathan's heart racing, a testament to the clandestine exchange they had been enjoying throughout the evening. Genevieve's presence had been a source of comfort and excitement, a reminder that they shared secrets and a deeper connection that set them apart from the rest of the world.

"Yes... Jonathan," she said a little awkwardly. That was probably going to take time to get used to. "And you must call me Genevieve."

As they exchanged glances and whispered words, Jonathan could not help but revel in the enchantment of the moment. Their shared world, rich with mystery and hidden treasures, felt like a place where anything was possible.

But when he dared to lift his eyes from Genevieve's, he was met with Lord Alastair Fitzroy's menacing stare from across the table. The intensity of Alastair's gaze cast a shadow over the evening, filling Jonathan with a creeping unease. How did he know this man? And why did he seem to have so much hatred for

Jonathan? That was another mystery on his hands, but he was not sure that it would have such a wonderful outcome when he unraveled the truth.

\*\*\*

After all the guests had departed and the grand mansion fell into a quiet slumber, Jonathan found himself restless and sleep deprived. The echoes of the evening's events lingered in his mind, and the mysteries that lay ahead weighed heavily on his thoughts. With the hour growing late, he sought solace in the flickering candle light of his study.

Seated at his ornate desk, he retrieved his sketch book and dipped his quill into the ink well. The cool night air whispered through the open window, carrying with it the subtle scent of lavender that had become synonymous with Genevieve. He could not help but find inspiration in that delicate fragrance, a reminder of the connection they had forged.

With every stroke of his quill, Genevieve's likeness began to emerge on the paper. He carefully captured the curve of her smile, the sparkle in her eyes, and the essence of her presence that had drawn him in to a world of secrets and adventure. Each line and shadow he added to the sketch was a reflection of the emotions and desires that had been simmering beneath the surface. He wanted to capture all of her, not just her beauty but what lay inside as well. Her wonderful personality that he truly did adore.

The candle light danced on the paper, casting intricate patterns of light and shadow across the portrait. As he continued to work, he could not help but feel a sense of intimacy with the image he was creating. It was as if he were baring his soul through his art, allowing his feelings for Genevieve to flow freely onto the canvas. Feelings he had not even properly acknowledged to himself as yet. Yes, he knew that she intrigued him, but beyond that he was not sure what he felt.

Hours passed, the candlewick slowly diminishing in size, and the sketch took on a life of its own. Genevieve's presence seemed to materialize before him, and he could not help but be captivated by the ethereal beauty that his quill had conjured.

By the time dawn's first light crept through the window, Jonathan had created a work of art that captured not only Genevieve's likeness but also the essence of their connection. It was a testament to the unspoken promises and shared secrets that had brought them together, a reminder of the adventure that awaited them on their journey into the heart of Grafton Moors.

As he gazed at the finished sketch, Jonathan could not help but wonder what the future held for them. The mysteries of the past were calling, and he knew that Genevieve and he were bound by something deeper than he had ever imagined. The portrait before him was not just a representation of her beauty; it was a symbol of the connection they had forged and the adventures that lay ahead.

# CHAPTER 12

The soft patter of winter rain against the window provided a soothing backdrop to the storm of emotions that raged within Genevieve. The cozy cocoon of her bed enveloped her, tempting her to linger in its warmth, but the memories of the previous evening's ball refused to let her slip into slumber.

The dance, the tantalizing revelation, and Jonathan's intense gaze all seemed to be etched into her mind, vivid and unforgettable. She could not help but replay the moments in her thoughts, each one a testament to the whirlwind of emotions that had stirred her heart.

As she lay in the dimly lit room, her eyes fixed on the rain smeared window pane, she felt a yearning to relive the enchanting moments from the night before. The connection she had forged with Jonathan was unlike anything she had ever experienced, a blend of excitement and mystery that had left her breathless. The revelation of their shared secrets, the promise of uncovering hidden treasures in the moors, and the warmth of his presence had all conspired to awaken something within her. It was a yearning for adventure and a connection that transcended the boundaries of their world. The fact that he seemed as connected to her family treasure as she was, only drew her closer to him. He was excited, just as she was, and he even had a journal in his own family library that talked of the treasure.

What did this mean? It was terribly intriguing and she could not wait to find out more. Now that she had the map and letter back, the journey could happen once more. That thought, mixed in with the memories of the night before, meant she could hardly drift off for even a moment. The pull of wakefulness grew stronger with every passing moment. The memories of the ball were like a siren's song, calling her to embrace the day and the uncertain future that lay ahead. With a sigh, she pushed back the covers and rose from her bed, determined to face whatever challenges and revelations the day had in store.

Genevieve stood before the ornate mirror in her chamber, her reflection gazing back at her in the soft light of the early morning. She was dressed in a simple, elegant night gown, and her hair, slightly disheveled from the night, framed her face like a cascade of silk. She could not help but wonder if she looked different than she had the night before, after everything that had transpired with Jonathan.

As she continued to gaze at herself, lost in thought, the door to her chamber opened, and Madeline, her faithful maid, entered the room. Madeline's presence was a gentle intrusion, a reminder that the world outside her thoughts still continued to move forward.

"Milady," Madeline said with a warm smile, "shall I assist you in getting dressed for the morning?"

Genevieve appreciated Madeline's presence, knowing that her maid's help was not merely about clothing but a comforting touchstone in the midst of her busy life. With a nod and a soft spoken "Yes, Madeline, thank you," she allowed her maid to help her select an outfit for the day.

Madeline, ever the patient and meticulous servant, helped Genevieve get dressed for breakfast. The rustle of fine fabric and the careful placement of every button and ribbon were familiar rituals that had been a part of her life for as long as she could remember. Her hands moved with grace, and her quiet presence offered comfort on this morning when her thoughts were anything but still.

With her attire impeccably arranged, Genevieve descended the grand staircase and made her way to the drawing room where her family had already gathered for breakfast. The scent of freshly brewed coffee and pastries filled the air, but her mind was preoccupied by the events of the previous evening and the choices she now faced.

She took her designated place at the table, feeling the weight of her cousin's expectant gaze upon her. Her piercing gaze held a silent question, one that demanded an answer. Genevieve knew that her actions the previous night had not gone unnoticed. The connection she had formed with Jonathan, the shared secrets, and the promise of adventure had all been born in the shadows of the ballroom. Now, she had to navigate the careful balance between the expectations of her family and the desires of her own heart.

Before Genevieve could even help herself to breakfast, Eleanor, with barely contained excitement, began to speak about the waltz. Her words spilled forth with a rush of enthusiasm, painting a vivid picture of the evening's most memorable moment.

"Genevieve, my dear," Eleanor exclaimed, her eyes sparkling with anticipation, "We simply must talk about the waltz! It was the most enchanting moment of the entire evening."

"What do you mean?" Genevieve asked, trying to feign innocence. Naturally, she was aware of her cousin's desire to indulge in idle conversation, yet she needed to maintain a composed demeanour.

"The music swirled around you two," Eleanor said, her voice filled with awe, "and it was as if the entire ballroom came to a stand still. All eyes were on the handsome duke and you, locked in a graceful dance that was pure magic. It was a moment that will be talked about for weeks to come."

Eleanor's words made Genevieve's heart race. The waltz had indeed been a transformative experience, one that had left an indelible mark on her. She exchanged a knowing glance with her cousin, acknowledging the significance of the moment, even as her mind wandered to the secrets and promises that had been shared on the dance floor. But still, the idea of gossip worried her. She did not wish to be the center of attention that way.

"It was merely a dance," she declared. "There were many dances of the night."

"Oh, my dear Genevieve," Eleanor said with a sly smile, disregarding all of her endeavours to diminish the significance of the dance, "you should have seen Lady Isabella's expression during the waltz. Her envy was practically written across her face."

Genevieve forced a polite smile, but the unease in her chest grew. Lady Isabella was usually a composed and sophisticated woman. The thought of her harboring envy, even if only for a fleeting moment, weighed heavily on Genevieve's mind. She could not help but wonder what Lady Isabella had seen during the waltz, what secrets her keen eyes had uncovered. The dance had been an intimate moment shared with Jonathan, and its magic had been undeniable. How many people had seen that?

Before Genevieve could defend herself further, her father spoke loudly, silencing everyone else. "I would like you all to know that we have received an invitation to a dinner being hosted by The Duke and Duchess of Cavendale happening later in the week."

The name of the esteemed hosts sent a ripple of anticipation around the table. The Duke and Duchess of Cavendale were renowned for their extravagant gatherings and their influential social circle. It was an invitation that held a promise of grandeur and sophistication. Genevieve's heart fluttered with a mixture of excitement and trepidation. The prospect of attending such a prestigious event was an opportunity that few could decline, but it also meant that she would have to see Lady Isabella again. And even worse than that, Alastair, the man whose menacing gaze had cast a shadow over her previous evening.

She felt her stomach twist into knots at the mere thought of facing him. The memory of their interactions, filled with tension and unspoken disapproval, lingered in her mind. It was a complex situation, one that she would need to navigate with care.

As her family discussed the upcoming dinner, Genevieve kept her unease hidden behind a polite smile. She knew that she could not let her reservations show, for the Duke and Duchess's invitation was an honor that she couldn't refuse. The grandeur of the event and the web of social expectations that surrounded her were inescapable, and she would have to face Alastair with grace and composure, regardless of the tumultuous emotions that stirred within her.

After the breakfast concluded, Genevieve found herself drawn to her bedchamber by an itching curiosity that had been gnawing at her ever since the ball. The memories of the waltz, the revelations, and the dance with Jonathan had left her restless, and the map she had received was a siren's call that she could no longer ignore.

She entered her bedchamber, the soft patter of rain against the window pane creating a calming sensation surrounding her, yet it also seemed to drum a rhythm of caution. The world beyond was cloaked in a veil of mist and mystery, a world of secrets hidden beneath the ancient moors of Graftonshire.

There, folded neatly on her dresser, lay the map, and it beckoned to her with a magnetic force that was impossible to resist. Its faded ink contained the promise of adventure and intrigue, and the call of the Grafton Moors was too strong to deny.

With hesitant fingers, Genevieve reached for the map. Unfolding it, she traced the faded lines and cryptic symbols with her gaze, wondering again about the secrets it held. The stories of hidden treasures and enigmatic clues danced in her mind, and she could not help but feel the pull of destiny. She had been yearning for this escapade and exhilaration, and now desired to immerse herself entirely once more.

She longed to reengage with the activity without delay. There were no hindrances she desired to impede her progress.

Genevieve was just about to reach for her cloak, her heart and mind consumed by the allure of the Grafton Moors and the mysteries that lay within when Madeline stepped into her bedchamber. The worry etched across Madeline's face was palpable as she saw what Genevieve was doing, and it was clear that she had concerns about her young mistress venturing out in to the inclement weather.

"Milady," Madeline began, her voice carrying a note of apprehension, "I must implore you to reconsider heading outside today. The weather is foul, and the roads will be treacherous. It is a folly to venture out on a day like this."

Madeline's words were filled with genuine concern, a reflection of her deep care for Genevieve's well being. The servant's loyalty and protectiveness were unwavering, and she was not one to stand by when she believed her mistress was making a risky decision. Genevieve paused, the words of her devoted maid weighing heavily on her. The window revealed a somber, overcast sky, the rain drumming a relentless rhythm against the panes. The thought of venturing out in such inclement weather was, indeed, a cause for hesitation.

She met Madeline's concerned gaze with a soft and appreciative smile. "I understand your worry, Madeline," Genevieve replied, "and I appreciate your concern for my safety. But there is something that compels me to go out today. It is a matter of great importance."

Madeline, though clearly worried, knew her mistress well enough to understand the determination in her eyes. Genevieve's sense of purpose was unwavering, and it was not a trait to be taken lightly.

"Very well, milady," Madeline said with a resigned nod, her concern giving way to a desire to support her mistress's decision. "I shall help you prepare, and I will make sure you are properly dressed to face the elements..."

Their conversation, however, was abruptly interrupted by the entrance of Harry. His sudden appearance drew Genevieve's full attention, and she could not help but wonder what had brought him to her bedchamber at this crucial moment. Did he have some kind of premonition that she was trying to escape? The anticipation in the air was thick, and she hoped that his arrival might offer some clarity or a new perspective on the choice that lay before her. There was an innate sibling intuition between them, a connection that told him something was afoot.

Inquiring with a curious tilt of his head, Harry's eyes met Genevieve's, and she could not help but feel her resolve crumble under his gaze. It was as if he could see right through her, sensing the turmoil that had been roiling within her since she had first laid eyes on the map.

Unable to withhold her intentions any longer, she decided to share her plan with him. "I am planning to visit the Seabrook Ruins once more."

As she spoke, she could not help but notice the mix of emotions in Harry's eyes. Apprehension was etched in his features, a concern for her safety and the perils of the unknown. Yet, there was also an underlying understanding, he knew that she wanted to hunt for treasure once more, even if she was not saying that.

Harry, always protective and caring, understood his sister's yearning for adventure and discovery. He had seen the spark of adventure in her eyes countless times, and he knew that, once her heart was set on something, she was determined to see it through.

With a sigh, he finally spoke, his words laced with both caution and support. "Genevieve, you know the Moors can be treacherous, especially in this weather. But I also know that your spirit is unyielding. If this is what you truly desire, I will stand by your side."

Genevieve was moved by her brother's unwavering support, his willingness to accompany her on a path filled with uncertainty and adventure. As they stood there in her bedchamber, their shared resolve gave them the strength to face whatever lay ahead in the enigmatic heart of Grafton Moors.

# CHAPTER 13

Jonathan sat at the head of the breakfast table, the soft chatter of his family around him fading into the background as his mind became captivated by memories of the previous evening. In his thoughts, he revisited the enchanting moments he had shared with Genevieve. He recalled the moment they had first locked eyes, their gazes drawn together as if by an invisible force. The music had swirled around them, and the ballroom had seemed to disappear, leaving only the two of them in a world of their own.

The touch of her hand as they had danced lingered in his memory, a gentle yet electrifying connection that had sent intense shivers down his spine. Their synchronized movements, perfectly attuned, had made it feel as if they were in a dance of their own making. As he relived these memories, a soft smile graced his lips, and his heart fluttered with the desire to see Lady Genevieve again, to share more of those magical moments on the dance floor. The enchantment of the previous evening remained etched in his mind, a compelling force that drew him back to the captivating Lady Genevieve. He knew that it was dangerous to have these thoughts, especially when he knew that he was closed off to love, but he could not get her off his mind no matter what he did. It was like she had all but consumed him.

Jonathan's mother, Rosalind, cleared her throat gently, her voice drawing him back from the depths of his reverie. With a soft, knowing smile, she had remarked, "Lady Genevieve Ellsworth and you made a splendid pair during the waltz last night, Jonathan. It was quite the sight."

Jonathan looked up, meeting his mother's gaze. He had offered a slightly sheepish but pleased grin. "Thank you, Mother. Lady Genevieve is an excellent dancer, and the dance was certainly a highlight of the evening for me. I had a very good time with her."

He knew that his mother might read in to this and make assumptions, but right now he wanted to talk about Genevieve. He could not seem to stop himself.

Rosalind's eyes had twinkled with maternal pride as she had added, "It seemed as if the two of you were in perfect harmony, as if you had danced together many times before."

Jonathan had nodded, a fondness in his eyes as he had thought of Genevieve. "It did feel that way, Mother. She is quite remarkable."

"The gown that she was wearing was very lovely. I hope you remembered to compliment her on it."

Truth be told, Jonathan was not sure if he had said anything about her dress. Genevieve and he had so much more to talk about. They were so busy discussing the map and the quest that Genevieve had embarked upon that nothing else mattered. Surely Genevieve knew that he thought she looked beautiful. Did he really need to tell her when he could not take his eyes off of her? Perhaps it would be better for him to make sure he told her the next time he saw her.

But before he could answer his mother, Agatha jumped in with her own opinion. She leaned in slightly and had remarked, "You know, Jonathan, Lady Isabella is truly a remarkable young woman. Her grace, her elegance, she would make an exceptional duchess, do you not agree?"

Jonathan raised an eyebrow, feigning casual interest, and had replied, "Is that so? Lady Isabella is certainly a fine lady, no doubt."

Agatha continued, her voice carrying the weight of her intentions. "Yes, and she comes from a family with a long standing history of maintaining their estates and holdings. It is a quality we should consider when thinking about our future, wouldn't you agree?"

Jonathan had kept his tone measured, refusing to be drawn into a direct conversation about his own future. He knew that he had a duty as a duke now, but he did not wish to be controlled. He needed to have some power over his life! "Of course, Agatha. A stable family history is indeed important."

Agatha's eyes flickered as she added, "You know, it is just a shame about Lady Genevieve and her... adventurous spirit. One might say it is a bit reckless, and certainly not befitting of a duchess. That is something I believe you should consider in future interactions." When Jonathan did not dignify this with a response, Agatha continued. "You know, Jonathan, there have been rumours about Lord Harry Ellsworth and an unfortunate incident with a horse which led to his limp, and how Lady Genevieve might have been to blame."

The revelation sent a ripple of unease through Jonathan. The thought of Genevieve being responsible for her brother's injury was unsettling, especially considering the connection he had formed with her. Jonathan's brow furrowed, and he regarded Agatha with a mix of surprise and concern. "An incident with a horse? What happened?" he inquired, his curiosity piqued.

Agatha's lips curled into a sly smile as she responded, "The details are rather hazy, and one can never be sure of the accuracy of such rumours, but it's said that her recklessness led to her brother Harry's injury. Some even suggest that it might have been avoidable if she had been more cautious."

Jonathan's heart almost stopped beating. He did not want to listen to this, he did not want to hear it when it might not have been the truth. He replied cautiously, "Rumours can be misleading, Agatha. We should be careful not to jump to conclusions based on hearsay. Lady Genevieve has proven to be a woman of character and integrity in my experience."

Agatha merely shrugged in response, her expression inscrutable. The shadow of suspicion hung in the air, casting a pall over their breakfast conversation. Jonathan did not like any of this, he had actually found himself captivated by Genevieve's bold spirit. That was something he truly admired about her.

Luckily at that moment, his mother changed the conversation, instead talking about the next social event they would all be expected to attend. Yet, as Jonathan, thought about the upcoming dinner at Cavendale Manor, his mind filled with a sense of anticipation. He could imagine the splendid setting and the prospect of seeing Lady Genevieve once more made his heart race. The idea of sharing more private moments away from the prying eyes of society was exhilarating. Perhaps that was not where his mind should have been wandering, but when it came to Genevieve, Jonathan was starting to understand that he would never have control over his mind.

\*\*\*

After breakfast, the familiar solitude of Jonathan's library beckoned him like an old friend. The oak paneled room, with its shelves of leather bound tomes and the scent of aged paper, had always been his sanctuary. Here, he found solace in the worlds captured within the pages of countless books, and today, it was not just any book that called to him, but his great uncle's journal once more.

The journal rested on a velvet cushion on the center table, its leather cover weathered and worn from countless journeys and adventures. The pages within were a testament to his great uncle's spirit of adventure, filled with tales of daring escapades, hidden mysteries, and elusive treasures. As Jonathan took the journal in his hands, he could not help but feel a connection to the great explorer, his uncle, whose footsteps he had always longed to follow.

Today, however, a particular section of the journal seemed to leap out at him, its words etched on the page like a whisper from the past. The section was about Grafton Moors, a place he had only heard of in passing, a place he had not yet been lucky enough to explore. The tales of the Moors were woven with threads of mystery and intrigue, tales of hidden secrets, and whispered legends of untold riches. It was a place that beckoned Jonathan from the pages of the journal, stirring something deep within him.

As he sat in the comfortable arm chair, his fingers gently traced the edges of the journal's page, feeling the texture of the paper beneath. The words seemed to dance before his eyes, and his mind was transported to a world of possibilities and adventure. Grafton Moors called to him, an urge to explore its hidden wonders and unearth the secrets that had eluded generations of his family. The urge to visit was almost as overwhelming as the memories of the previous night with Genevieve.

Without hesitation, he made up his mind. The pull of Grafton Moors was too strong to resist. He rose from the armchair, his heart pounding with anticipation. The library's warmth, the scent of aged books, all seemed to fade into the background as he prepared to venture out into the world beyond, into the embrace of the chilly winds and the looming clouds.

He donned his warmest coat and gathered the essentials: a sturdy leather satchel, a lantern, a compass, and a small collection of his uncle's maps. With every step, he could feel the excitement building, the call of the Moors growing stronger. As he opened the heavy wooden door of the library and stepped into the cold embrace of the day, he could not help but smile. The unknown awaited, and the adventure had just begun.

This was the closest he had felt to his ancestors from the past ever, and that was exciting. Perhaps this was not the same as exploring the ocean, but it was surely going to be wonderful.

Upon reaching the Moors, a vast expanse of wild and untamed land, Jonathan could not help but marvel at its beauty. The open landscape, shrouded in mist, held an air of mystery and adventure. The very same aura that had called to him from the pages of his great uncle's journal. He could see the words written in the journal coming to life in front of him. The people living in the world might have changed over the years, but nature remained the exact same.

As he ventured deeper in to the Moors, the cool breeze ruffled his coat, and the distant call of a bird echoed through the air. But what truly captured his immediate attention was a figure in the distance. A silhouette against the moody sky that sent a jolt of recognition through him. It was Lady Genevieve, a fellow seeker of mysteries and hidden treasures, a kindred spirit in the world of adventure. Who would have thought? Every time he explored his new surroundings, fate put her in his path, which really was amazing.

Genevieve stood there, her posture exuding the same determination and spirit that he had grown to admire. Her wavy blonde hair flowed gently in the breeze, and the rugged terrain seemed to pose no challenge to her. The Moors had not tamed her; instead, she stood as a testament to its wild beauty and allure.

Jonathan's heart, which had often been composed and level headed, now quickened its pace. The sight of her, here in this remote and enigmatic place, filled him with a rush of emotions. There was a sense of connection, an unspoken bond forged through shared experiences and the thrill of discovery. They were two kindred souls brought together by the call of adventure, and seeing her again only added to the anticipation of what lay ahead. He was going to speak to her, he knew that, but just for a moment he wanted to watch her from a distance to admire her. It did not matter to him what Agatha had said about this woman, he felt like he understood her more than most and there was a reason that he was endlessly captivated by her. It was because she was beautiful and exciting, different to anyone else he had met in his life. No one else could ever compare.

# CHAPTER 14

The Grafton Moors stretched before Genevieve, a winter wonderland adorned in frost and sporadic flakes of snow. The air was crisp, carrying the scent of pine and the hushed whispers of the moors. Against this picturesque backdrop, a familiar silhouette caught her attention, making its way through the vast expanse.

As the figure drew nearer, the distinctive features began to emerge, revealing the unmistakable form of Lord Jonathan... *again!* He seemed to be everywhere that she was. His silhouette cut through the winter landscape, and a sense of anticipation stirred within Genevieve. What brought him to the Moors on this cold and enchanting day?

She quickened her pace, the crunch of frozen earth beneath her boots echoing in the stillness. The Grafton Moors seemed to hold their breath, as if aware of the impending encounter between two souls drawn together by a shared curiosity.

Jonathan, wrapped in a coat against the winter chill, turned to meet her gaze as the distance between them closed. His eyes, a reflection of the moody sky above, held a warmth that contrasted with the frost-kissed surroundings.

"Lady Genevieve," he greeted, a hint of a smile playing on his lips. The name carried a melody, a connection that seemed to resonate in the quiet expanse of the moors. He dipped his head in a bow, following society rules which seemed far too formal for Genevieve these days. Although of course she returned a curtsy as she greeted him too.

"Your Grace," she replied, her voice soft and filled with curiosity. "What brings you to the Grafton Moors on this wintry day?"

He gestured towards the landscape around them, a canvas painted in shades of white and gray. "I found myself drawn to the beauty of this place. There is a certain magic in the air, do you not think?"

Genevieve nodded, a shared appreciation for the mystical allure of the Moors passing between them. The winter landscape, though cold and unforgiving, held a unique charm that seemed to deepen their connection. They got so lost in one another for a moment, that Genevieve forgot her brother was with her. Until he spoke.

"We are here because our grandfather's map has brought us this way. We are adventuring some more."

"Lord Harry, it is good to see you, as always."

Harry seemed to ground both Genevieve and Jonathan, stopping them from getting too lost in the memories of what it was like to hold one another and to dance together. That was probably for the best, because it felt like a fairy tale was surrounding them. Anything could happen when it seemed like they were dancing in the pages of a novel.

"How very exciting," Jonathan agreed. "I would love to join you, if that suits. As I have been saying to Lady Genevieve, my great uncle also wrote about the Graftonshire treasure, so I believe he knew a lot about it as well."

Harry caught Genevieve's eyes, and thankfully took her nodding well. "That sounds very good, Your Grace. Let us walk some more."

As they walked together through the winter landscape, the frost crunching beneath their boots, Genevieve could not shake the sense that this encounter on the moors was a continuation of a dance — one that held the promise of uncharted territories and the unraveling of secrets yet to be discovered.

Guided by the intricate details on the map and her grandfather's enigmatic letter, Genevieve, Jonathan, and Harry ventured deeper into the heart of the Grafton Moors. The landscape unfolded before them like a mystical tapestry, each step revealing a new layer of the untold story hidden within the moors.

Their exploration led them to an unassuming stone, standing alone amidst the frost kissed landscape. At first glance, it appeared to be just another element of the moors' natural decor. However, as Genevieve drew closer, her keen eyes caught a delicate, almost obscured engraving on the stone's surface — a riddle waiting to be unraveled.

"Look at this," she exclaimed, her fingers tracing the faint lines of the engraving. "It is a riddle, hidden in plain sight. What do you think this means? Do you think this is where the map is leading us? It certainly seems very strange. Could it have simply been sitting here for years?"

Jonathan and Harry gathered around, their eyes focused on the stone. The anticipation in the air was palpable as Genevieve read aloud the cryptic words etched in to the weathered surface. *"In the shadows where waters flow. Beneath the moon's enchanting glow. Seek the heart, a stone's throw. Where River whispers grow."*

"What could that mean?" Jonathan asked, both of them turning towards Harry as if he was the one who held all the answers.

"*Shadows where waters flow* could hint at concealed passages..." Harry pondered. "And the *moon's enchanting glow* maybe means looking for something at night time. But the river... what river could it be? That is the part I am struggling with."

"The closest river to here is the River Lox, is it not?" Jonathan asked, showing a surprising knowledge for the area he had just moved to. "Do you think that could be the *river whispers*? I can not quite fathom what that part of the clue might be referring to"

Genevieve's heart beat a whole lot faster. She knew the River Lox well, and now that she was really thinking about it, she had also heard a lot of tales about the whispering trees that surrounded the area, every fairy tale suggested as much. It really did seem like this was what the clue meant.

Since this was the first real clue Genevieve had understood, and the next part of her adventure, she could hardly contain her excitement.

"Oh my goodness," she exclaimed happily, pressing her hand to her chest in glee. "I believe that you are right. I think we need to go to the river next."

She could not wait. Genevieve felt more alive than she had done in a very long time. Now she was more convinced than ever that this was exactly what she was supposed to be doing.

Harry's voice, usually steady and resolute, took on a touch of anxiety as he suggested, "Perhaps we should make our way back. The cold is becoming quite biting."

Genevieve had to admit that the winter's chill, unforgiving and relentless, began to seep through the layers of their attire. The landscape, though enchanting, carried a bite that penetrated the very fabric of their exploration. But she did not wish to leave right away.

Lost momentarily in her musings, Genevieve nodded absentmindedly. The allure of the River Lox and the mysteries it held had momentarily eclipsed the biting reality of the winter's embrace. If this was just about her, then she would continue, but she could not allow her brother to keep on going. The cold would never be good for his leg.

As they retraced their steps, the hidden patches of ice beneath the snow posed an unforeseen challenge. It was a lot harder to walk. All of them had to be so careful with their footing. Genevieve was so focused on her brother that she hardly realized where she was putting her own feet. She did not even think to look down to check where she was placing her feet...

"Oh my!" she gasped as she started to realize her fatal mistake.

Because of this, her heart nearly stopped beating the moment her foot slid out from underneath her. The world started to spin and a dizziness threatened to consume her. Genevieve panicked, but before she could fully register her impending fall, the unforgiving ground rushing to meet her, Jonathan's hand reached out with lightning speed.

His warm grasp closed around her arm, catching and steadying her with an effortless strength. The contrast between the ambient cold and the warmth of his touch sent a shiver down her spine, setting her heart aflutter.

"Careful there," Jonathan said, a playful smile dancing in his eyes. The closeness of the save lingered in the winter air, an unspoken acknowledgment of the fragility of the moment.

"Thank you, Your Grace," she gasped as she clung to him while he rose her back to her feet once more. "I appreciate it."

Grateful for the steadying support, Genevieve met his gaze, her eyes reflecting a mixture of surprise and appreciation. The winter's chill may have tried to assert its dominance, but Jonathan's intervention had provided a respite, a reminder that even in the harshest of environments, the warmth of connection could be found. Her chest warmed up, Genevieve felt like she was sitting in front of a roaring fire instead of out in the snow.

When the trio reached the edge of the Moors and it was time to part ways, Jonathan expressed his excitement to continue on with this adventure.

"Once the winter releases its hold," Jonathan mused, his gaze fixed on the distant horizon, "we can embark on a new chapter of our journey along the River Lox. There's much to uncover, and I believe our combined efforts will unveil the mysteries that lie in wait."

His words carried a sense of determination and shared purpose, and Genevieve found herself nodding in agreement. The prospect of exploring the River Lox with Jonathan, the person who had become an integral part of her adventure, filled her with a renewed sense of enthusiasm.

"Yes, I believe together we will be able to unravel any clue there. Whatever the *river whispers* have to say."

Sadness washed through Genevieve as she said her farewell to the duke. His lovely smile and the kindness in his eyes were a welcome, beautiful sight that she knew she could get used to. She did not know when the winter chill would let up and allow them to travel to the river. She did not know when she would have a chance to see Jonathan again, but she hoped it would not take a long time. As she watched him walk away, her heart fluttered with anticipation.

However, before the siblings started their own walk home, Harry's usually light hearted tone took on a somber note. He clearly had something important he needed to tell her.

"Genevieve," Harry began, his expression carrying a weight that echoed the gravity of his words. "We must be cautious with you spending so much time with a gentleman, particularly when it involves a Duke. The intricacies of societal expectations can cast shadows on reputations, and yours is delicate, to say the least."

His reminder, though delivered with concern, brought with it the chill of reality. Genevieve nodded, acknowledging the complexities of their situation. The thrill of exploration, the shared excitement with Jonathan, was tempered by the awareness that their pursuits could be scrutinized through the lens of societal expectations.

"Harry," she replied, her voice carrying a reassuring warmth, "I understand the delicate nature of my reputation. Rest assured, our adventures will always be undertaken together, as a united front against whatever challenges may arise. I will not do a thing to tarnish our name."

Harry nodded, but he seemed a little uncertain. Like he was not convinced that Genevieve would do the right thing. She supposed the only thing she could do was prove it to him over time. No matter how much she enjoyed the presence of the duke, and how her heart fluttered at the mere sight of him, this was all about their grandfather's map and nothing more. She would simply have to be careful not to look at him for a moment too long again.

As they walked home through the fading light of the winter day, the thrill of the day's discoveries merged with contemplative musings on the intricacies of societal expectations. Genevieve could not shake the sense that their journey, intertwined with the pursuit of hidden treasures and the unraveling of mysteries, walked a delicate tightrope between the expectations of society and the calling of adventure.

# CHAPTER 15

In the dimly lit confines of his study, Jonathan found solace amidst the pages of his uncle's weathered journal. The antique lamp cast a warm glow over the aged parchment, illuminating the intricate details of the tales of hidden treasures, and the mysterious hints about Grafton Moors that filled its pages.

Meticulously, he studied the faded ink, his eyes tracing the contours of each word as if deciphering a secret code. The journal, a tangible link to his family's past, held within its pages the echoes of adventures long gone. Jonathan's fingers traced the edges of the worn leather cover, feeling the weight of history in his hands.

With the journal spread open before him, he juxtaposed its contents with the clues he had sketched on a rough map. The lines and symbols on the map seemed to come alive in the flickering light of the lamp, forming a tapestry of possibilities. It became increasingly clear that the hidden treasure, spoken of in legends and guarded by the shadows of the past, may not be a simple myth, and that his adventures with Genevieve and Harry might really lead them somewhere.

He grew excited at the prospect of finally making his way to the River Lox to see what was there. Finding the stone with the words carved into it was an exciting turn in this adventure, and Jonathan was thrilled to see what the *whispering river* could hold for them.

He had to admit, he also could not wait to see Lady Genevieve again. Her pretty face and her lovely smile. Plus the way that she looked deep into his eyes as if she could *really* see him in ways that he was not expecting...

In the midst of his contemplation, the door creaked open, and Jonathan looked up to find Lucas entering the room. Lucas observed him with a mixture of curiosity and concern, his eyes lingering on the worn pages of the journal and the map that he was sketching.

"You are busy, Jonathan," Lucas chuckled as he took a seat beside his friend. "What on earth are you working on here?"

Jonathan closed the journal for a moment, his eyes meeting Lucas's. "Legends of hidden treasures, uncharted territories," he replied, his voice carrying a hint of both wonder and uncertainty. "The kind of tales that captivate the imagination, whether they turn out to be truth or myth."

Lucas leaned back, studying Jonathan with a knowing gaze. "Distraction, then?" he ventured, sensing that there was more beneath the surface.

Jonathan nodded, a faint smile playing on his lips. "A welcome one," he admitted. "In the pursuit of these mysteries, the burden of the present momentarily eases."

"You can remain as distracted as you want, dear Jonathan, but soon you will have to adjust to being a duke." Lucas paused thoughtfully for a moment. "I know you love to adventure, but this is no longer life on the open waters. You must adjust to life on land sooner or later."

Jonathan sighed heavily. "Yes, I do understand that, but I can not just shut that side of myself down. No matter what title I have inherited. I will always want to adventure."

Lucas, attuned to the weight that memory placed on Jonathan's shoulders at the mere mention of the ocean, broached the subject with a gentle touch. "Jonathan," he said, his voice soft yet firm, "there are regrets that chain us to the past. But dwelling on them will not change what has already transpired. You must find a way to move on with your life and to find happiness elsewhere. Perhaps life on land will suit you more than you expect. If you give it a chance."

Jonathan's gaze dropped, acknowledging the truth in Lucas's words. The tragic voyage, a specter that haunted his thoughts, seemed to loosen its grip, if only slightly. The shadows on the parchment mirrored the shadows in his soul, but perhaps, as Lucas hinted, it was time to let go of the regrets that tethered him to that fateful event. The journey in to the mysteries of Grafton Moors held the promise of not just hidden treasures but also the chance to untangle the knots of the past that bound him.

That was something he was not expecting, but if he could loosen the tight knot in his chest, then he would love that. If this adventure could give him a new lease of life, which was something he very desperately needed.

"Thank you, Lucas. Your words mean a lot to me. I will try and move on."

As the weight of personal history hung in the air between Jonathan and Lucas, a gentle reminder of the evening's commitment broke the contemplative silence. The clock on the wall ticked away, marking the passage of time as the shadows in the study seemed to lengthen.

Before they could delve any deeper into the intricacies of their past, a sense of duty pulled at them — the commitment to a dinner at Cavendale Manor. The prospect of an evening in the company of others beckoned, diverting their focus from the shadows that lingered in the corners of their personal histories. Jonathan was even going to have to put the Grafton Moors and the River Lox out of his mind for a little moment. Until the morning at the very least.

"Lucas," Jonathan began, his voice carrying a note of acknowledgment, "it seems duty calls before we can dive further into our shared history. Cavendale Manor awaits. We must get dressed and prepare ourselves for a night with the ton."

Lucas nodded in agreement, a shared understanding passing between them. The weight of the past would linger, but for now, they stepped out of the study and into the corridor, leaving the shadows behind. The promise of an evening at the Cavendale Manor beckoned, where the layers of society and the complexities of their personal histories would intertwine, at least for a while.

\*\*\*

The grandeur of Cavendale Manor welcomed Jonathan and Lucas as they stepped through its imposing doors. The Duke and Duchess of Cavendale, gracious hosts, extended warm greetings to all their guests. The opulence of the manor was evident in every detail, from the intricate chandeliers to the exquisite tapestries that adorned the walls. It was wonderful.

"Ah, Your Grace, you are here!" Lady Isabella caught Jonathan quickly, giving him all of her attention the moment he stepped through the doors. She was making it very obvious that he was the only one in her eye line, by ignoring Lucas. "It is wonderful to see you. Thank you for attending."

Jonathan forced himself to smile. He knew that Agatha wanted him to be polite to Isabella. In fact, she wanted him to court her, and to go on to marry her. But Jonathan could not fathom up interest in this woman. Beautiful as she was, she did not spark excitement within him in the same way that Genevieve did.

Jonathan knew that he was going to have to carry on the conversation though, it would be rude not to. "Lady Cavendale, how are you enjoying the evening?"

Her response was a suggestive twirl of a lock of her hair. "Oh, it is positively enchanting, especially with such charming company around."

The not so subtle hint in her words hung in the air. Jonathan shifted uncomfortably, trying to maintain a courteous distance while not meeting Lucas's eyes. He could talk to his friend about this later on. "I am glad that you are enjoying yourself. Your family has created quite the atmosphere for a dinner party."

Isabella took a step closer, her proximity becoming more pronounced. "You know, Your Grace, seeing the moon lit sky from our gardens is just magical."

"I am sure." Jonathan nodded slowly, starting to wonder how he was going to escape this. "It is truly a nice night. The carriage ride over here showed us as much."

Undeterred, Isabella let out a melodious laugh, her fingers lightly grazing Jonathan's arm. "Would you like to take a walk with me? I could show you."

Jonathan maintained his polite demeanor, though his desire for distance was growing. "Lady Cavendish, I appreciate the sentiment, but I prefer to enjoy the festivities from the side lines tonight. I would much rather remain inside."

Her eyes, filled with determination, held Jonathan's. "Come now, Jonathan. Do not be so serious. A little walk will not hurt. It shall be fun."

As the music swirled around them, Jonathan felt the need to extricate himself from the situation. "I do not think so. I would not like to go outside before I have had the chance to talk to everyone. It is my duty to mingle as the new Duke of Graftonshire."

She pursed her lips, a flicker of disappointment crossing her face. Lady Isabella was not impressed, but there was nothing else she could do. He had made his feelings very clear, whilst also trying to be polite. "Well, if you change your mind, you know where to find me. I shall also be greeting our guests for the evening."

With that, she sauntered away, leaving Jonathan with a sense of relief. He glanced at Lucas who had a raised eyebrow and a knowing smile playing on his lips. He looked like he was trying his hardest to stifle his laughter at the complicated mess Jonathan found himself in. But Jonathan soon realized that Lady Isabella was going to be the least of his problems tonight. He found himself caught off guard by the unmistakably hostile glance that met his gaze. Lord Alastair Fitzroy, standing at a distance, regarded him with an intensity that spoke volumes. The air seemed to crackle with tension, and Jonathan could not help but wonder about the source of Alastair's animosity.

*What have I done?* He wondered as he forced his eyes away from Alistair. *Why must he look at me that way...*

However, the lingering tension from Alastair's hostile glare seemed to dissipate the moment that Genevieve and her family entered the opulent halls of Cavendale Manor. The enchanting melody of the evening shifted, and Jonathan's attention pivoted, momentarily forgetting the shadows that had cast their pallor over the gathering.

Genevieve's entrance was nothing short of radiant. The delicate fabric of her lavender colored gown caught the light, and her grace eclipsed the grandeur of the surroundings. In that moment, the dance of social intricacies and unspoken hostilities faded into the background, and Jonathan found himself spell bound by her presence. She truly was the most beautiful woman he had ever laid eyes on. It was hard for his heart to stop pounding like crazy as he looked at her. His whole body lit up, like he was one of the candles himself. How had he never felt such an intense wave of emotion before? What had Lady Genevieve done to him?

Any intention he may have harbored of addressing the lingering hostility with Lord Alastair Fitzroy evaporated as he watched Genevieve move through the room. Her laughter echoed like a melody as she greeted the other guests of the evening, and the flicker of candle light played upon her features, highlighting the grace that seemed to emanate effortlessly from her.

In the midst of societal expectations and the complexities of the evening, Genevieve's arrival became a beacon of light, momentarily eclipsing all else. The shadows that had clung to the corners of the gathering seemed to retreat in the face of her radiant aura. As their eyes met, Jonathan felt a warmth that transcended the cold stares and unspoken tensions that lingered in the background. The grandeur of Cavendale Manor, with its elaborate tapestries and polished chandeliers, faded in to the periphery. For Jonathan, the true spectacle was Genevieve, a vision of radiance amidst the shadows, inviting him to step into a dance where the only steps that mattered were the ones taken towards her.

# CHAPTER 16

As Genevieve entered the resplendent drawing room of Cavendale Manor, a hushed anticipation filled the air. The elegant ambiance, with its ornate furnishings and soft glow of candle light, seemed to be in harmony with the sophisticated assembly gathered within. It was just as lovely as she was expecting it to be, and she was looking forward to what the night might hold.

Amongst the crowd, her eyes sought a familiar presence. One she had been worried she might not see again for a long time, until she remembered the dinner party tonight. And there, standing amidst the grandeur, was Jonathan. Just the man she had wanted to see. The room, filled with animated conversations and the gentle hum of societal niceties, momentarily blurred into the background as their eyes locked.

In that fleeting second, everything else seemed to fade away. The tapestries on the walls, the chandeliers casting a warm glow, the genteel murmur of voices — all paled in comparison to the intensity of the gaze exchanged between Genevieve and Jonathan. There was no one else in the world who could make her feel that way, that could make her heart race like crazy. She actually pressed her hand to her chest in the hope that she might calm herself down somewhat. She did not wish to have blushed red cheeks right now. The connection, though brief, held the weight of shared moments and unspoken understandings. It was a glimpse of familiarity in the midst of societal intricacies, a silent acknowledgment that transcended the constraints of decorum. Genevieve felt like this man understood her more than anyone else could.

She only wished that she could cross the room directly to speak with him, to block out the rest of the guests at the dinner, so they could talk about the River Lox and what was next on their adventure, but of course she could not. Not when duty expected her to greet everyone who was in attendance. Perhaps later, she would get her chance to speak with just him.

Of course she could not be seen alone with him tonight. Not with Harry's warning words still floating through her brain.

Genevieve glided through the lavish surroundings of Cavendale Manor's drawing room, a symphony of sensory delights enveloping her. The soft hum of conversations created a melodic backdrop, weaving through the air like a delicate sonata. The room was adorned with the rich aroma of fragrant blooms, their perfume mingling with the laughter and polite exchanges.

Chandeliers cast a warm glow, illuminating intricate wall patterns that seemed to dance with the flicker of candle light. The opulence of the setting, however, was secondary to the current of thoughts that coursed through Genevieve's mind.

Her senses, attuned to the refined elegance of the evening, were preoccupied with a singular question — did Jonathan remember their secret promise about the River Lox? Amidst the grandeur and societal expectations, her thoughts reached out, like tendrils searching for a familiar echo. He promised that he would adventure with them to find the next clue on the map trail, and she really prayed that was something that he wanted to do.

As Genevieve took her place at the dinner table, the opulence of Cavendale Manor's dining room surrounded her. The polished silverware, delicate crystal, and the glow of candle light created a tableau of refined elegance. Yet, amidst the setting's grandeur, a discordant note played in Genevieve's heart.

Her hopeful musings about the secret promise of the River Lox were disrupted by the unavoidable presence of Lady Isabella. Seated next to Jonathan, Isabella's gleeful expressions and shared smiles felt like tiny jabs to Genevieve's heart. It was almost as if she had arranged the seating like this on purpose, to be closer to Jonathan and to upset Genevieve. It was very obvious that Jonathan did not know what was happening, but politeness dictated that he talk to his neighbor, especially since her family were hosting this dinner. So each whispered exchange between them echoed with a resonance that seemed to amplify the growing sensation of jealousy within her.

She did not want to be jealous, but she could not stop this green snake of irritation and upset from rising within her.

With each passing moment, the yearning to converse with Jonathan intensified. She longed to ask him about the map, the hidden treasure, and the enigmatic River Lox. Yet, the intricate dance of societal expectations dictated the course of the evening, leaving Genevieve to navigate the complexities of unspoken emotions and concealed desires. She was seated next to her brother, so she could have talked with him about their adventure, but Harry could not give her the answer that she needed.

The dinner, though a tableau of refined harmony, became a battleground of emotions for Genevieve. The whispers of hidden treasures and shared adventures seemed drowned out by the clinking of silverware and the laughter that echoed through the grand dining room. Amidst the opulence, the yearning for a private conversation with Jonathan lingered, a desire that mirrored the dance of shadows and light in the intricate patterns of the room. Her appetite was naught; she could scarcely partake of sustenance, so it was a relief as the meal started to come to an end.

The dinner concluded, and the ladies gracefully retreated to the drawing room, Genevieve felt a subtle yearning for the serenity of the night air. She did not wish to listen to gossip about people she did not care about, and knew that she would be dragged into a conversation should she attend. The grandeur of Cavendale Manor's terrace beckoned, and she succumbed to the impulse, stepping into the cool embrace of the night. So, as soon as she got a moment to do so, she slipped away from the crowds to escape the pressure that was crushing her.

Images of Isabella and Jonathan at the dinner table, talking to one another flooded her mind and made her feel incredibly sad.

The quietude enveloped her, a stark contrast to the lively murmur of the drawing room. Lost in her thoughts, she gazed at the moonlit expanse, its silvery glow casting gentle shadows on the terrace floor. The night held a tranquility that seemed to echo the unspoken desires of her heart.

In the midst of her contemplations, the soft sound of approaching footsteps interrupted the stillness. Startled, she turned around, and her heart raced as her eyes met Jonathan's. The very man that she had been thinking of. There, under the canopy of stars, their connection felt palpable all over again. All the jealousy she had been feeling at the dinner table dissipated in to nothingness. Surprise curled up in her mouth, and he met her smile with the same look.

"How are you?" Genevieve asked as soon as Jonathan stood beside her, leaning on the balcony under the starlit sky. His warmth spread through her, making her smile widen.

"I am looking forward to a moment of peace. It has been quite a long night already."

"Dinner was lovely, the hosts are very kind."

If Jonathan wanted to make any comments here about his time with Lady Isabella, and how captivating her conversation was, it would be now. Genevieve's shoulders rolled up as panic got the better of her. She needed to know how he truly felt, but she also was not sure if she could handle it. Her whole body tensed up and her heart stopped beating as she waited for him to speak. To end this painful anticipation.

"I have been thinking a lot about our quest, you know," Jonathan declared, flooding relief through Genevieve. Not only did he not want to talk about Lady Isabella, but he wanted to talk about their adventures, which was just the thing that Genevieve wanted to discuss. "And I can not imagine what we will find at the River Lox."

Genevieve laughed. "It is a mysterious place that I used to visit a lot when I was a child. It is beautiful. I am sure we will have a great adventure when we go."

"The weather seems favorable; perhaps we could explore the River Lox soon. I am sure, like me, you do not wish to wait too long."

Genevieve's heart quickened with excitement. "Soon? That sounds like a promising plan. I can not wait to see what secrets it holds. I keep wondering what we are going to find. If it will be another stone with an engraved message or something else."

"The map might lead us to the treasure, and we shall be rich," Jonathan laughed and Genevieve could not help but join in. He was making light of this, but having fun as well, which only made her feel better and even more excited about it all. "Perhaps tomorrow morning will be the perfect time for us."

She was very grateful to have Jonathan on her side. Harry too, of course. She was not ever going to forget that her brother had helped her through everything. But Genevieve could not deny that her heart skipped a beat at the idea of spending more time, closer with this man. The enigmatic duke who she still wanted to know more about.

The terrace, with its cool night breeze and the faint murmur of distant laughter from the drawing room, became a cocoon for their shared dreams. In the hushed tones of their conversation, Genevieve sensed the promise of a journey yet to unfold — a journey that transcended the confines of societal expectations and ventured into the uncharted territories of their intertwined destinies. Excitement flowed through her veins at the thought of what was to come.

"Ah, Genevieve, I have been looking for you. I thought you might be in the drawing room, but you are here."

The ethereal spell was abruptly shattered by the approach of familiar footsteps. Harry's voice cut through the night, the soft cadence of his words breaking the cocoon of their private world. His shadow loomed before he fully stepped into view, and in his eyes, Genevieve found a silent understanding — a mix of concern and caution.

"I believe we are needed back inside, my dear sister. There are people looking for you. You do not wish to be missing for too long."

The weight of their positions in society, the delicate dance of reputation and propriety, became all too clear. The uncharted territories they longed to explore were constrained by the expectations that bound them. If only the rest of the world did not exist, they could be free to talk and enjoy themselves as much as they wanted.

"Of course, Harry." Genevieve hated that her beautiful moment was about to be destroyed, because with Jonathan she was having the nicest time she'd had all evening. But she knew that her brother was right to worry about her reputation. This was something that she needed to be more concerned about as well, not that it was the easiest thing in the world to do when her heart simply wanted to remain with him. "I shall come right away. I just wanted to get some air, that is all. But I am feeling much better now."

"It was lovely talking with you," Jonathan declared as he bowed at the pair. "Lady Genevieve and Lord Harry, I do hope that you enjoy the rest of your evening."

"You too," Genevieve replied with a curtsy in return. Her heart hurt as she pulled away from Jonathan, but she knew it was the right thing to do. "See you soon."

Following Harry back inside, Genevieve carried the bitter sweet residue of the evening with her. The longing for a world beyond societal constraints, the secrets shared under the stars, and the thrilling anticipation of what lay ahead left an indelible imprint on her heart.

The terrace, now bathed in the soft glow of moon light, held the echoes of their conversation. The unspoken promise lingered, suspended in the night air, as Genevieve re entered the drawing room, where the grandeur of Cavendale Manor enveloped her once again. The secrets and dreams shared on the terrace became fragments of a puzzle waiting to be completed, and the journey, though momentarily interrupted, remained poised on the brink of discovery.

# CHAPTER 17

Alistair had spent countless evenings within the opulent walls of Cavendale Manor, where grandeur and elegance danced together in perfect harmony. Yet, tonight, the air held an electric charge, a promise lingering in every shadowed corner. The familiar hum of conversations and the melodic clink of glasses intermingled, creating a symphony of celebration that seemed to echo through the lavish halls.

Perhaps tonight would be the night that he would finally find a woman to marry, and a woman who could help to solve all of his financial problems.

However, after a few conversations with the ladies in attendance of the night, Alistair needed a moment to himself, to gather himself back up again and to recall what he was there for. He needed to make sure the women he spoke to were financially suitable, so he did not waste any time.

Seeking a moment of respite, Alistair stepped out on to the terrace. The night sky stretched above him, adorned with a myriad of stars, and a gentle breeze carried whispers of secrets untold. As he inhaled the crisp air, he felt the weight of the evening lift momentarily from his shoulders.

However, the tranquility was short lived, shattered by the clandestine exchange of hushed voices. Alistair's instincts, honed by years of navigating the intricate web of high society, guided him towards the source. Lady Genevieve and the new duke, Jonathan, two figures silhouetted against the ambient glow of the manor's windows, engaged in an earnest conversation. Again. Why did he only ever see the pair of them together? The two people who ruined his life. He hated to see them happy and talking like they had done nothing to him.

The words *treasure* and *River Lox* floated to Alistair's ears, a combination that stirred a dormant curiosity within him. The mere mention of potential riches sharpened his senses, transforming the terrace into a stage for a clandestine drama. If they knew where treasure could be found, then Alistair wanted to know. Perhaps that way he would not need to worry about getting married for money. *If* there was a treasure to be found, then he needed to find it. He needed to know more.

His footsteps, though purposeful, were silent as he edged a little closer, trying to pick out every word. Shadows concealed him, allowing him to eavesdrop without detection. Genevieve's voice carried a note of excitement, and Jonathan's responses were measured, hinting at the gravity of their discussion which only made him believe more that there really might be something out there. Alistair's keen intellect began to weave the fragments of information together, creating a tapestry of intrigue. The River Lox, a place well known but seldom discussed in such clandestine tones, was either holding a treasure or a clue towards it.

It was only when Lord Harry Ellsworth stepped out onto the terrace that the conversation halted, disappointing Alistair. He ducked and hid while everyone else slipped inside the building, barely letting out a breath until he was completely alone.

*My goodness,* Alistair thought once he was confident enough to stand once more. But as he allowed his eyes to shut, he found himself ensnared in the tendrils of his own memories. The memory of the biggest tragedy of his life, which meant he definitely deserved this treasure far more than Jonathan. That man was responsible for killing Trevor, among with a lot of other people. He did not deserve happiness with money as well. Nor did Genevieve. Her rejection still stung him when he really thought about it.

He let the rush of memories consume him for just a moment. The ship, proud and resolute, battling against the unforgiving sea, came vividly to mind. Alistair could almost taste the salt on the air and feel the deck beneath his feet as the ship sailed towards an inevitable fate. The end of his best friend's life.

The memory, though haunting, was not new to Alistair. The turbulent waters, the ominous clouds that painted the sky, and the heart wrenching loss of lives — all etched in to the fabric of his being. The bitterness of resentment, simmering beneath the surface, now surged forth with renewed intensity.

No one needed to die that day. Alistair would never forgive Jonathan for that. The burden of that day weighed heavily on his shoulders, and the resentment that had festered over time threatened to consume him. There was no way he could let

Jonathan find a treasure, it would not be fair to Trevor and the others.

Alistair smiled to himself, certain that this night had just given him the answers he needed. Now all he had to do was find out more about the River Lox and what clues might be there. Since he could not ask either Jonathan or Genevieve, he was going to have to find someone else who might have some ideas.

With a calculated grace, he headed back inside and approached the Duke of Cavendale, who held court amidst the lavish surroundings. Alistair exchanged general pleasantries, his demeanor composed yet subtly charged with an underlying determination. The Duke, unaware of the currents beneath the surface, welcomed Alistair into the ongoing conversation with a genial nod. Alistair engaged for a little while, before he subtly guided their conversation toward the heart of his current interests — the captivating region and, more specifically, the mysterious River Lox. The more he found out, the better equipped he would be to find this treasure.

"Your Grace," he began, his tone casual, "Graftonshire is renowned for its breath taking beauty and rich heritage. It is a region with tales to tell."

The Duke, pride evident in his demeanor, nodded. "Indeed, Lord Fitzroy. Graftonshire holds a tapestry of stories, each thread woven into the very fabric of its landscapes."

Alistair raised his glass in agreement, concealing his true intentions behind the veneer of polite conversation. "I have heard whispers of a river that weaves through this enchanting county. River Lox, if I recall correctly? Is that somewhere you have spent a lot of time."

The Duke's expression shifted subtly, a nuanced acknowledgment. "Ah, River Lox," he replied, a touch of nostalgia in his voice. "A river that has witnessed centuries unfold. Its waters are said to hold the echoes of forgotten tales and untold secrets. There are many stories surrounding that river. You must have heard a lot of them when you were younger."

Leaning in, Alistair, his interest genuine but carefully veiled, inquired further. "Such rivers often become the stuff of legends. I wonder, Duke Cavendish, if you might share some of the tales associated with River Lox. A man of your stature surely has insights into the hidden corners of Graftonshire. If I have heard stories about this river when I was younger, then I do not recall."

The Duke, pleased by the opportunity to recount the lore of his homeland, began to share stories of River Lox — its meandering course through ancient woodlands, the tales of mystical creatures said to inhabit its banks, and the folklore passed down through generations.

"It snakes through Graftonshire like a silvery ribbon, its waters carrying the whispers of ages past. Legend has it that the river's source lies deep within the heart of the ancient woodlands, a place untouched by the hands of time. That is why the trees are thought to whisper. Because they have never been damaged by humans."

Alistair listened attentively, his interest genuine as he absorbed the details. "That is fascinating."

The Duke continued, "The locals say that River Lox has a spirit of its own — a guardian of the land. In the moonlit nights, some claim to have heard melodic murmurs rising from its waters, as if the river itself is telling stories to those who would listen."

"Please," Alistair said with a smile. "Tell me more."

The Duke's words painted a vivid picture of a river steeped in mystique. "The banks of River Lox are adorned with ancient stones, each bearing the weight of centuries. It is said that these stones mark the passage of time, bearing witness to the ebb and flow of Graftonshire's history."

Alistair, captivated by the information he was getting here, prompted the Duke to share more. "And are there specific landmarks along the river that hold significance?"

The Duke nodded, a knowing gleam in his eyes. "Indeed, there is a spot known as Serenity Bend, where the river takes a gentle turn, revealing a hidden alcove shaded by ancient willows. It is a place of tranquility and natural beauty, often frequented by locals seeking solace or inspiration. Oh, and then there is the Whispering Glen," he continued. "A secluded glade where the river's current seems to carry the secrets of the world. Locals often visit the Glen, believing that the murmurs in the air hold answers to life's mysteries."

The Duke, unsuspecting and wrapped in the charm of conversation, provided morsels of information that Alistair eagerly absorbed. Each detail, no matter how seemingly trivial, was a puzzle piece in Alistair's quest for understanding. The currents of the River Lox, its twists and turns, its hidden secrets — all began to take shape in his mind.

"And have you heard anything about treasure?" Alistair asked, hoping that he could sound innocent here. Not that he was looking for anything.

The duke laughed. "Oh my, yes. Many a man has driven himself insane looking for treasure."

"How funny." Alistair laughed lightly. "I can only imagine."

Alistair's demeanor remained composed, his expressions betraying nothing of the intricate web he wove with each carefully crafted question. The parlor, adorned with elegance and refinement, became the setting for a silent exchange of information, a dance of words that held the promise of uncovering hidden treasures. He appreciated every part of what he was being told here, and he knew that it would take it with him on his brand new mission.

The evening at Cavendale Manor progressed in a whirl of laughter, music, and the clinking of crystal glasses. Yet, for Alistair, the festivities were but a kaleidoscope of colors obscuring the intricate maze of plans and strategies that churned relentlessly in his mind.

His interaction with the Duke of Cavendale, the unsuspecting harbinger of information, drew to a seemingly casual conclusion. Alistair raised his glass in a toast, the crystal catching the ambient light in a dazzling display. To the onlookers, it was a gesture of camaraderie and celebration, but in Alistair's mind, it was a silent acknowledgment of a future yet to unfold.

As the cool liquid touched his lips, Alistair's thoughts were far from the present revelry. In that moment of shared pleasantries, he toasted to more than the night's festivities. It was a toast to a future of triumph, a future where the treasures of the River Lox would be within his grasp. The clink of glasses resonated like a bell tolling the beginning of a calculated pursuit.

Retribution, too, found its place in the silent toast. The resentment that had long simmered within him now bubbled to the surface, and Alistair envisioned a day when the scales of justice would tip in his favor. The treasure, a means to an end, would not only secure wealth but also serve as a vessel for revenge against Jonathan and Genevieve.

As the night wore on, and the echoes of laughter mingled with the strains of music, Alistair moved through the crowd with a sense of purpose that belied the facade of social congeniality. The evening was a masquerade, and he, the orchestrator of a clandestine symphony, continued to weave the threads of his plans with every step.

In the grandeur of Cavendale Manor, where opulence and intrigue coexisted, Alistair's mind raced ahead to a future shaped by his calculated endeavors. The night, with all its charm and allure, became the backdrop for a silent oath — a vow to seize the treasure and, in doing so, rewrite the narrative of his past with a pen dipped in the ink of triumph and retribution.

# CHAPTER 18

The estate awoke to a picturesque scene, a world transformed by a blanket of fresh snow that adorned every tree branch and roof. The morning sun cast a soft, golden glow over the landscape, turning it into a winter wonderland.

Inside the drawing room, the warmth of the crackling fire contrasted with the frosty tableau outside. Agatha, the lively storyteller, wove animated tales about Isabella that flowed effortlessly through the air. Her words painted vivid pictures, occasionally punctuated by Lucas's thoughtful nods as he absorbed the narrative.

"...she is such a lovely lady. So glamorous all the time, she will make quite the wife one day."

However, Jonathan found himself detached from the lively atmosphere, his attention elsewhere. He knew that his cousin was trying her best to get his attention, but he just could not give it. Especially in a conversation about a woman he had no interest in. His breakfast sat mostly untouched, a mere backdrop to the flurry of thoughts that occupied his mind. Agatha's tales, once a source of delight, now seemed distant and inconsequential.

Rosalind, ever perceptive, noticed her son's preoccupation. With a mother's intuition, she playfully attempted to draw Jonathan back in to the present. "Jonathan, dear, what do you think about Lady Ellsworth? She is such a charming young woman, whom you appear to like very much. I have always admired her spirit and grace. Do you think she adds a delightful touch to our gatherings?"

Jonathan managed a half smile in response to his mother's comment, the gesture a feeble attempt to reassure her of his engagement. The words registered, but Jonathan's thoughts lingered on the unspoken complexities that surrounded him. The mention of Genevieve, the woman with whom he had shared hushed conversations about hidden treasures and the River Lox, added a layer of tension to the morning. He knew he could not talk about her in front of his cousin, because Agatha had made her preference for Lady Isabelle very clear.

The snow outside, pristine and untouched, mirrored the facade of composure Jonathan maintained. Yet, beneath the surface, a storm of conflicting emotions continued to rage. He knew he needed to escape from the stern and inquisitive gazes surrounding him, so as soon as he could leave, he headed for the library which had become something of a safe haven for him.

The library, with its rich tapestry of knowledge and the comforting scent of aging paper, provided a haven for his troubled thoughts. As Jonathan sank in to the embrace of a worn leather chair, the hushed ambiance enveloped him, offering a momentary escape from the complexities that lingered outside.

But he was not alone for long. His best friend seemed to sense that Jonathan was struggling with his emotions and it was not long before he appeared to join Jonathan. The creak of the door announced his presence, and as it closed behind him, the library seemed to cocoon them in a shared understanding.

"This is the perfect place for hiding out," Lucas teased lightly as he took his own seat. "I am sure you can embrace all your distractions in here."

Jonathan smiled thinly. "Sometimes, I just need a break from the expectations that are always weighing upon me."

Lucas narrowed his eyes in a perceptive gaze. "You seem troubled, my friend. Something on your mind? Are you thinking about your treasure hunting some more?"

Jonathan sighed, the weight of the world pressing down on him. "I am, but I am also thinking about Lord Alistair Fitzroy. The way that he looked at me last night with such hatred, it has me wondering where those feelings might have come from. There is something about him — familiar, yet elusive. Like a puzzle I can not solve however hard I try."

"I see." Lucas frowned. "Lord Fitzroy does have a way of weaving mystery around him. What is it that bothers you? He might look at everyone in that manner."

"No, there is something there. I am sure of it. It is like a sense of deja vu, but I can not place it. And there is this unease about his behaviour. I feel like it is solely focused on me, but I can not work out why. Nor is he approachable enough for me to simply talk with him about it. Especially since we only cross paths at society events. We can not talk openly and honestly there for fear of causing a scene."

"Yes, that can be a problem. Unfortunately, I do not know enough about him, Jonathan. About his past and history to help you."

As the conversation unfolded, Lucas's gaze momentarily drifted to the sketch book that lay open on the table. A glimpse of Genevieve's unfinished portrait adorned the pages, capturing her essence in delicate strokes of pencil. Jonathan, catching the shift in focus, felt a flicker of vulnerability. The unfinished portrait mirrored the uncertainty of their current situation, a reminder of the secrets and desires that lingered beneath the surface.

He hoped that Lucas would not ask him about the portrait, or the woman he had been drawing because he did not know what he would say. He did not have any answers for his friend, least of all how he was feeling. That was something he had not worked out yet for himself.

Sensing the unspoken turmoil, Lucas deftly diverted the topic, much to Jonathan's relief. "Well, I am sure you have a lot that you need to do here. I do not wish to get in the way of your distractions. Plus I do need some time to pen some letters."

With a subtle nod and a silent understanding, he excused himself from the library, leaving Jonathan to the solitude of his thoughts. Jonathan could not stop himself from staring at the portrait, and trying to work out why his pulse was pounding so heavily as he looked in to her beautiful, drawn eyes which were so clear it was like looking right into her soul.

He knew that they had discussed heading to the river this morning, but with the snow falling he was sure that she would not want to. But Jonathan could not bear the weight of his thoughts any longer. The turmoil within him begged for release, and the solace of the outdoors beckoned like a siren's call. With a determined spirit, he mounted his horse, a loyal companion in times of both joy and distress, and directed it toward River Lox. Just to see if there was anything worth traveling the distance for.

The soft touch of falling snowflakes created a serene ambiance, a stark contrast to the storm raging within his mind. Each flake seemed to carry a whisper of tranquility, but Jonathan found no solace in their delicate dance. The rhythmic sound of hooves against the snow covered ground echoed his restless thoughts.

As he neared the river, a peculiar sight interrupted his introspection. Distinct footprints marred the pristine canvas of snow. Jonathan halted his horse and dismounted, his eyes fixated on the trail. The footprints bore the mark of intention, leading a mysterious dance across the frozen landscape. Kneeling beside the tracks, Jonathan traced their path with gloved fingers, searching for clues that might reveal the identity of the mysterious visitor. A knot tightened in his stomach as the realization dawned — the footprints were recent.

Someone was here.

A chilling sensation crawled up his spine, as if unseen eyes bore witness to his every move. He straightened up, glancing around the snow blanketed expanse. The world seemed hushed, nature holding its breath in anticipation. The only sound was the distant murmur of the river, a constant companion in Jonathan's moments of reflection.

His gaze narrowed, scanning the surroundings for any sign of the observer. The snow clad trees stood sentinel, their branches weighed down by the burden of winter. No figure emerged from the shadows, no presence revealed itself. Yet the unease lingered, a phantom in the air. Jonathan, now acutely aware of the isolation, felt the need to dispel the disquiet that hung heavy around him. He remounted his horse, casting one last wary glance over his shoulder.

The journey continued, each hoof beat accompanied by the echo of unanswered questions. The river, frozen in time, mirrored the uncertainty that gripped Jonathan's heart. Seeking solace, he rode deeper in to the winter landscape, hoping to leave behind not only the foot prints in the snow but also the unsettling feeling of being watched.

The biting chill in the air settled like the unease that nestled in the pit of Jonathan's stomach. Despite the pressing mysteries of the footprints, his attention shifted to the river's edge. There, much to his surprise, stood Genevieve, a beacon of light dulled by some unseen shadow. Her usual radiance, like the sun on a crisp morning, was replaced by a subtle darkness that clung to her features.

She must have realized that it was a mistake to come in this weather, and that she might be about to get herself into trouble once more. But as always, Jonathan would not let her fall.

Harry, steadfast and vigilant, stood close by her side, a silent guardian watching over her protectively. His eyes, usually filled with warmth, now held a hint of concern that matched Jonathan's own. The trio formed an unspoken tableau against the backdrop of the snow covered landscape, each figure a puzzle piece in a scene of quiet turmoil.

Jonathan urged his horse closer, the soft crunch of snow beneath its hooves punctuating the stillness. As he dismounted and approached Genevieve, he noted the furrowed lines on her forehead, the telltale signs of inner conflict. Her gaze, usually bright and lively, carried a weight that spoke of a burden he could not fathom. She was usually such a delightful ray of sunshine. What had her looking so different now? Jonathan did not like the pain in her face one bit.

"Lady Genevieve," he called softly, a gentle inquiry woven in to the syllables of her name. She turned to him, a fleeting attempt at a smile tugging at the corners of her lips. The melancholy in her eyes, however, betrayed the facade.

Harry acknowledged Jonathan with a nod, his eyes silently conveying a shared concern. The unspoken question lingered in the air — what troubled Genevieve? Did she believe he was not coming? Or perhaps she had searched and had been unable to find a clue under the blanket of snow covering everything. If that was the case, then they could simply return when the day was better. When the weather allowed them to. It did not need to be such a heart breaking moment, even if it was disappointing.

Jonathan did understand why she might be frustrated and upset. He had never liked it when his own journeys on the ocean were disrupted by the weather, which might have been why he decided to sail on that fateful day.

Jonathan's curiosity tugged at him, and he could not suppress the urge to understand the source of Genevieve's distress. "Is everything alright?" he inquired, his voice carrying a genuine concern. "Has something happened? Is there anything that I can do?"

Genevieve sighed, a soft exhale that seemed to release a fraction of the burden she carried. "I do not know what to say, Your Grace. We have been here for a while now, and we have discovered something. But it is not good news, I am afraid."

Harry nodded in a sad agreement, but he did not offer any more information. It seemed that he was going to have to wait until Genevieve was ready to talk.

A sadness overcame Jonathan even though he did not know what was happening. Just seeing Genevieve's eyes flooded with hurt broke his heart a little. Whatever he needed to do to make that look slide away from her face, he would do it.

# CHAPTER 19

The cold wind whispered through the air, grazing Genevieve's cheeks and momentarily diverting her attention from the tempest of hurt swirling within. The winter landscape, adorned in a pristine blanket of snow, seemed to echo the quiet turmoil she could not escape. Harry stood beside her, a silent pillar of support, but even his comforting presence could not shield her from the weight of the discovery they had made.

Her gaze found Jonathan's, his approach steady and gentle, like the falling snowflakes that danced in the air. His eyes, a reflection of concern and genuine care, met hers, and for a moment, the world stood still. The truth she had uncovered loomed large, casting a shadow on the serenity of the snowy scene.

A tear, unexpected and unchecked, traced its path down her cheek. She felt the vulnerability of that solitary tear, a silent messenger of the turmoil within. She tried to mask the storm behind a smile, a feeble attempt to reassure Jonathan and Harry, but she knew the facade was as transparent as the winter air.

Jonathan drew nearer, and Genevieve's heart fluttered with a mix of gratitude and trepidation. In his hand, a folded handkerchief, a small yet profound gesture of comfort. The unspoken offer hung in the air, a delicate thread connecting them in this moment of shared vulnerability.

As he extended the handkerchief, their fingers brushed — a fleeting touch that sent an electric pulse through Genevieve. It was as if the snow covered ground beneath them held its breath, acknowledging the subtle shift in the dynamics of their connection. The world seemed to blur for an instant, leaving only the awareness of his warmth against the winter chill.

Genevieve accepted the handkerchief with a grateful nod. Jonathan's presence, a beacon in the midst of emotional tumult, offered a solace she had not realized that she needed.

The frigid air clung to Genvieve's breath as she inhaled shakily, trying to steady the storm within her. Jonathan's concerned eyes bore in to hers, a silent inquiry that implored her to share the weight of the burden that had cast its shadow on her soul.

The cold wind bit at their faces, and as Genevieve drew in a shaky breath, Jonathan's eyes probed hers, silently urging her to share what weighed on her mind.

"Genevieve, what happened?" he asked, his concern etched in the furrow of his brow.

Taking a moment to steady herself, Genvieve began, "About an hour ago, Harry and I were studying my grandfather's map. We were engrossed in deciphering the symbols when we found something unexpected." Her fingers traced the contours of the map, a tangible link to the shared pursuit.

Jonathan leaned in, his gaze unwavering.

"We found a note, tucked among the rocks," she continued, her voice betraying a mix of frustration and determination. "It was a menacing ultimatum, imposing us to retract ourselves, a threat against our pursuit of the treasure."

Jonathan's features shifted in an instant. Concern twisted into anger, and a resolute determination settled in his eyes. Genevieve handed him the letter, so that he could read it for himself.

*To those who seek the treasure of Grafton Castle. Cease your pursuit, for the shadows you disturb hold more than riches. This land bears the weight of secrets best left undisturbed. The river whispers warnings, and the stones remember oaths long forgotten. Turn away now, for darker forces lie in wait. The treasure you seek is not worth the price that may be exacted. Let the echoes of this warning guide your steps, or face the consequences of your relentless pursuit. A Guardian of Graftonshire.*

The ink seemed to seethe with malevolence, each word a venomous warning etched into the paper. Genevieve watched with bated breath as Jonathan took these words in. Would he be as worried as Harry, and also want to give up the adventure, when it felt like it was a more vital journey than ever before?

"We can not let this threat deter us," Jonathan finally declared, meeting Harry's gaze. "If anything, it makes our quest feel even more like something we should do. We can not let someone else find the treasure, when we do not know what their intentions are."

Genevieve gasped, noticing Harry's deflating body language as it appeared that Jonathan was on her side.

"We should not let anything stop us," Jonathan declared, his voice echoing with a new found resolve. "Especially this."

"I agree," Genevieve affirmed, feeling a sense of strength in their unity. "I think that this is something we should continue on with as well."

She turned to Harry, who only nodded in agreement. Although he did not seem convinced with the journey, he was supportive enough to allow Genevieve to continue, as long as Jonathan would do the same thing. He had made it clear that he never intended to leave them alone, which was for the best.

"Look, Genevieve," Jonathan began, his voice carrying a warmth that resonated with hope, as he pulled a sketch book from his bag. "There is so much we have not explored yet. Hidden passages, uncharted corners — it is like a puzzle waiting to be solved."

Genevieve's gaze followed his pointing finger, tracing the lines of a drawing unlike anything she had ever seen before. She was entranced, amazed by his work. This was clearly something that Jonathan had created himself and it was absolutely stunning. She wished that she could find the right words to express her emotions, but a silence overcame her. She was too stunned to speak. Instead, she continued to follow Jonathan's finger along the drawing that outlined the majestic castle. Areas he emphasized became beacons of potential, each stroke of his pencil a promise of undiscovered realms.

"This tower here," Jonathan gestured, "we have not set foot in. And this corridor, it leads to a section we have barely touched. So even if the weather makes outside pursuits challenging, I do not think this is an area that we should ignore. The words in my great uncle's journal suggest that the castle is incredibly important."

As his words painted a vivid picture of unexplored territories, the weight of the threatening note began to lift. The castle on the paper transformed from a mere destination into a living, breathing entity, whispering tales of hidden chambers and forgotten mysteries. A spark of excitement flickered within Genevieve, a response to the dedication woven in to the lines of the sketch. Grafton Castle, once a static landmark, now pulsated with the heartbeat of their shared adventure. There was a lot more that they could do, and that thrilled her.

"I never realised how much there is left to discover," she admitted, a smile tugging at the corners of her lips.

Jonathan's eyes gleamed with a shared enthusiasm. "Our journey is far from over, Genevieve. The castle holds more secrets than we can imagine."

"Perhaps this is a good time for us to head home," Harry interjected, breaking the magic of Genevieve's special moment with Jonathan. "If there is more to be discovered inside, then this might not be the weather to be exploring the River Lox."

Much as it disappointed Genevieve, she knew that her brother was right. They had been searching for a clue in this area for a long while now and had not been successful. With the snow continuing to fall, it was not going to get any better.

"Yes, perhaps we should," she agreed.

"I have my horse with me," Jonathan said. "If you would like to ride with me."

Harry instantly looked at his sister, answering before she could, making sure his desires were known. "Yes, Genevieve, you should ride with the duke."

She wanted to argue, and insist that Harry ride to protect his leg, but she could see the determination in his eyes. She knew that it would not do good to argue with him when he was in this mood. Plus she knew he would be very upset with her if she brought up his leg. So, with Jonathan's help, she mounted the steed and clung to his back to stop herself from tumbling off as the horse started to trot along the snow.

Harry walked ahead of the horse, making sure the journey was not too quick. He did not seem too pleased by what had just transpired, but that did not stop Genevieve from smiling to herself. She basked in a sense of quiet satisfaction. The fact that Jonathan was on her side, and agreed with her, made her feel wonderful. She felt closer to him than she ever had before. Who knew if there really was something to be found at the castle, but she was thrilled to find out.

The journey back to Genevieve's home was marked by the hushed beauty of the falling snow. Jonathan's protective presence lingered, a reassuring warmth in the midst of winter's embrace. As they approached the familiar surroundings, the anticipation of reaching shelter and warmth took hold. Soon she would be indoors, and away from the biting cold.

Jonathan's hands, strong and steady, assisted Genevieve's descent from the horse. The brief touch sent a familiar thrill coursing through her body, a connection that transcended the physical act. It was a dance of unspoken understanding, a shared language that spoke of mutual care and trust. It was a feeling that she never wanted to let go of.

Almost immediately, the snow draped world around her yielded to the sight of Genevieve and Harry's father at the entrance of their home. His eyes, a mixture of relief and profound worry, met Genevieve's. The unspoken language of a parent's concern needed no words. As she stood there, the snowflakes settling in her hair, she felt the weight of his worry. Panic consumed her also because she knew that if he had seen the duke holding her hand then there would certainly be ramifications.

This was exactly what Harry had been trying to warn her about.

"Genevieve," her father called, his voice cutting through the tranquil air. His arms enveloped her in a tight embrace, a silent reassurance that she was home and safe. "And Harry too, I have been so worried about you. This is not the weather to be out in the elements."

"I am fine, Father," Genevieve replied, her words muffled against his shoulder. The concern in his eyes, however, lingered. "We are fine. The duke kindly helped us to return home."

Genevieve's father's gaze shifted to Jonathan. Their eyes met in a silent exchange, a conversation of unspoken understanding. "I see. That is very kind of you, Your Grace."

"It was no trouble," Jonathan said with an easy smile.

The wind picked up speed, howling through the air, which caused worry to flash across Genevieve's father's face once more. "Your Grace," he began, his tone firm yet caring, "you must stay with us for a while. You can not leave right now. It looks like the snow storm is imminent, and it is too risky to venture out. If the snow does not subside, you must stay the night with us. I would not be able to forgive myself if you left in this weather."

Genevieve's heart skipped a beat with excitement. She tried her hardest not to let it show, but the prospect of spending more time with Jonathan thrilled her. She would be able to talk with him as much as she wanted, if he decided to stay.

"Thank you, that is truly kind," Jonathan nodded in agreement, acknowledging the wisdom in her father's words. "I would appreciate some shelter."

"I shall get one of the stable boys to take your horse, and to leave it in our stables for now."

What a day this had turned out to be. Genevieve no longer had the threatening note, it was now tucked in Jonathan's pocket, but even that could not bother her if Jonathan was going to remain at her home all night long. There was no telling what would happen next...

# CHAPTER 20

The soft, diffused morning light filtered through the curtains, casting a gentle glow on the unfamiliar surroundings of Ellsworth Manor. As Jonathan roused from a night of restless sleep, memories of the previous day flooded back, momentarily disorienting him. The realization that he was in an entirely different place than his own home settled in, and he took a moment to orient himself.

The room, though elegantly furnished, felt foreign, each piece of furniture a silent witness to the history of Ellsworth Manor. The events of the day before played out in his mind like a vivid tapestry — the discovery of the threatening note, the shared resolve against the impending snow storm, and the quiet camaraderie with Genevieve and her father.

Amidst the unfamiliarity, one thought anchored him — the presence of Genevieve. The image of her, strong and determined, resonated in his mind, a beacon that cut through the haze of the unknown. The shared adventures, the unspoken connections, and the subtle touches that marked their journey together thrilled him in ways he was not expecting.

As Jonathan rose from the bed and made his way to the window, the morning light revealed the snow covered landscape outside. The world beyond the glass seemed quiet and serene, a stark contrast to the flurry of emotions that had accompanied their pursuit the day before. The world was still now, the storm over and done with.

He supposed that he would have to return home soon, but for now he wanted to thank his hosts for allowing him to stay.

Once dressed, Jonathan navigated the unfamiliar halls of Ellsworth Manor, the thought of Genevieve guided him like a compass. He could not wait to see her this morning, he was more excited to head to breakfast than normal, and deep down he knew that was because of her. He ached to see her smile, to feel her warmth, and to maybe hear her laugh once more.

The aroma of freshly baked bread and the rich scent of brewing tea wafted through the air as Jonathan descended the stairs to join the breakfast gathering. The table was a tableau of warmth and familial camaraderie, a scene that echoed the history embedded in the walls of this grand estate.

But the moment they spotted him, all family members greeted him warmly, making him feel more welcome than he expected. The Ellsworth family truly were wonderful people.

As he took his seat, every glance, every shared smile, and every unspoken word painted a picture of connection. Eleanor's anecdotes danced through the air, and the Ellsworth family queries filled the room with the gentle murmur of morning conversation. Yet, amidst the lively atmosphere, Jonathan's attention gravitated toward Genevieve always. He could not seem to help himself. Something kept pulling his eyes her way, no matter how hard he tried.

Every accidental lock of their eyes sent a subtle tremor through him, a heart beat that leaped a tad more than he cared to admit. Genevieve, with her grace and determination, became the focal point of his awareness. The nuances of her presence became vivid details etched into his memory. Her fingers, delicately holding the teacup, seemed to move with a grace that transcended the simple act. The flutter of her eyelashes, the soft curve of her lips when she smiled — all became details that he could not help but notice, each nuance etched into his consciousness forever. He knew that he would not be able to forget anything about her, ever.

"So, Your Grace," Genevieve's father began, a genial smile playing on his lips, "tell us more about your family. I understand you come from a long line of historians."

Jonathan, sipping his tea, met the man's gaze. "Yes, indeed. My family has a deep rooted passion for history. My late uncle was particularly fond of unraveling the mysteries of the past, and I find myself following fascinated by his writings."

Eleanor, chiming in, added, "It is fascinating how the love for history can be passed down through generations."

Before anyone could say anything else, the footman entered the room with a letter for the head of the household. Everyone waited in deep anticipation to find out what was inside, even Jonathan despite this not being his family. In the moment, it really did feel like he belonged here.

"Ah, I see," he declared with a smile. "It seems that the Winter Ball has finally been arranged. It shall be held in the village inn."

This news rippled through the air, igniting a palpable wave of excitement. The mention of the ball resonated with the promise of festivities and shared moments. The prospect of a winter celebration, with the village adorned in the splendor of the season, fueled the energy at the table. Jonathan even found himself thrilled by the idea of a dance. The prospect of seeing Genevieve in a ball gown sent his heart racing even faster. The image of her, adorned in the elegance of a winter ensemble, unfolded in his mind like a scene from a story book.

He knew that he was not supposed to be getting too close to anyone, or allowing anyone in to his heart, but he could not seem to stop Genevieve from making her way into his feelings, no matter how hard they tried. He caught her eyes across the table once more, and was thrilled to see the joy in her face also. Would they dance once more? He could not wait to have her that close to him again. He adored dancing with Genevieve in a way that he never expected to.

As the morning unfolded, the enchantment of the impending winter ball hung in the air like a delicate promise. The grandeur of the event, the twinkle of lights, and the joyous anticipation painted a vibrant picture in Jonathan's mind. However, eventually, the realization of the outside world gently nudged its way in to Jonathan's consciousness. It was time for him to depart from Ellsworth Manor, much as he had enjoyed himself and wished to stay.

He thanked his hosts profusely, so grateful for them for keeping him safe from the storm, and he took his horse from the stable boy once more. He was greeted by a transformed landscape. The snow, which had veiled the world in a pristine white blanket, now glistened in the soft glow of winter sun light. The storm had subsided, revealing a serene and untouched canvas that stretched as far as the eye could see. The snow would not last for long now, so he admired the beauty while it was there.

The crunch of snow beneath the horses hooves echoed in the quiet stillness, and Jonathan could not help but feel a tug of reluctance. The wish flickered within him — a desire that the storm had lasted just a little longer, allowing him to linger in the warmth of Ellsworth Manor and the shared moments that had unfolded within its walls. Being that close to Genevieve was truly wonderful. He had truly enjoyed every moment of it.

As Jonathan finally approached the door to his home, the realization of reentering the outside world settled in. The enchantment of Ellsworth Manor began to fade, replaced by the quietude of his residence. The door swung open, revealing the familiar surroundings of the drawing room. His mother, seated by the window, looked up at his entrance, her expression a mix of relief and concern.

"Where have you been?" Rosalind demanded. "I have been so worried about you."

"I apologise, Mother. I was invited to stay at the Ellsworth Manor to avoid the snow storm, once I took Lady Genevieve and Lord Harry home."

"I see." Rosalind's eyes widened. "That is unexpected."

He tried his hardest to avoid her gaze because he knew that she was bound to have a lot of questions about his feelings for Lady Genevieve. That was not something he wished to discuss right now. "I am fine, Mother. You do not need to worry so much."

Her concern, though subtly masked, lingered in the air. Jonathan could sense the weight of the worry she had carried in his absence. "But you were fine? At the Ellsworth Manor?"

Jonathan grinned. "I was looked after very well, thank you. I had a nice time with the family. They were truly kind to me. But now, I think I should rest."

His mother nodded at him, letting him leave, but Jonathan did not head for his bed chambers. He needed to rest but not sleep. He wanted to spend time in the familiar warmth of the library once more. But this time, he was not going to be alone from the very start. Lucas was already there, as if he was waiting for him.

"Ah, Jonathan, you have returned," Lucas said with a smile. "I have been worried about you. Where have you been?"

Jonathan repeated the story, telling his friend that he took Lady Genevieve and Lord Harry home, before he was invited to stay. "I thought it better than facing the storm outside."

"Wise," Lucas replied with an understanding nod. "But what were you doing at the River Lox in the first place? Did that have something to do with your treasure hunt?"

"It did, yes, but we actually found something troubling while we were there." Jonathan frowned to himself, the memory of the note weighing heavily upon him. "A threatening note, trying to prevent us from continuing on with our pursuit."

"You did?" Lucas looked stunned. "What did it say?"

Lucas's request hung in the air, a quiet yet insistent plea. Jonathan could feel the weight of the letter pressing against his chest, a tangible reminder of the ominous message that Genevieve and Harry had unearthed at River Lox. With a sense of reluctant determination, he withdrew the folded parchment from his pocket, unfolding it carefully. The words, stark against the aged paper, seemed to carry a weight beyond their ink.

"*To those who seek the treasure of Grafton Castle,*" Jonathan began, the very act of uttering the words drawing the room in to a hushed stillness. Lucas's eyes, filled with a mix of curiosity and apprehension, remained fixed on the letter. "*Cease your pursuit, for the shadows you disturb hold more than riches. This land bears the weight of secrets best left undisturbed. The river whispers warnings, and the stones remember oaths long forgotten. Turn away now, for darker forces lie in wait. The treasure you seek is not worth the price that may be exacted. Let the echoes of this warning guide your steps, or face the consequences of your relentless pursuit. A Guardian of Graftonshire.*"

The room seemed to hold its breath, the weight of the words lingering between Jonathan and Lucas. The letter, a cryptic message from an unknown Guardian, cast a veil of uncertainty over the treasure quest. He could sense Lucas absorbing the gravity of the warning, his expression mirroring the conflict of emotions within himself. Reading those words out loud actually held a gravity that reading them to himself did not. Jonathan had to admit, the threat felt very real.

Lucas broke the silence, his voice steady yet tinged with concern. "A Guardian of Graftonshire," he mused, his eyes narrowing as if searching for hidden meanings in the cryptic words. "Do you think this is a genuine warning or a tactic to dissuade treasure hunters?"

Jonathan considered Lucas's question carefully, the letter still cradled in his hands. "I am not sure," he admitted, the uncertainty lingering in the air. "But there is a weight to these words, a depth that goes beyond a mere deterrent. It is as if the Guardian is cautioning us about something more profound than the treasure itself. Do you think this is something that we should be troubled about?"

In the quietude of the library, the weight of the note became a shared burden, and with Lucas by his side, the shadows of uncertainty seemed to retreat, if only for a moment. The sketches and notes of his late uncle's journal, once a portal to a world of adventure, now became a road map to navigate the threats that lurked in the shadows of Grafton Castle.

# CHAPTER 21

Later that afternoon, the winter sun light filtered through the curtains of Genevieve's room, casting a warm glow. The grandeur of Ellsworth Manor surrounded her, creating a backdrop of timeless elegance. The anticipation of the grand winter ball lingered in the air, and with a mixture of excitement and nerves, Genevieve approached the mirror.

Her fingers delicately traced the intricate patterns of the deep blue gown that adorned her. The fabric, rich and luxurious, whispered with each movement, a symphony of elegance that resonated in the quietude of her room. The gown, carefully chosen for the occasion, embraced her form, accentuating the grace that seemed to radiate from within.

As she gazed at her reflection, the mirror unveiled a version of herself that felt both powerful and beautiful. The deep blue hue of the gown complemented the warmth of her skin, creating a contrast that emphasized the intensity of her eyes. The intricate details of the dress, from the fine embroidery to the gentle sweep of the fabric, painted a portrait of sophistication.

The excitement of the impending ball pulsed through her veins, and a soft smile graced her lips. Madeline secured a stray curl with a jeweled hair pin, her touch gentle yet purposeful. The grand winter ball was not just an event; it was a culmination of the unexpected winter that she had experienced. Genevieve's thoughts lingered on the prospect of seeing Jonathan again, the memory of their adventures together adding an extra layer of anticipation. The idea of his presence, his laughter echoing through the festivities, sent a thrill through her.

Every adjustment Madeline made, every delicate touch, seemed to heighten the sense of occasion. The room, adorned with the warmth of Ellsworth Manor and the subtle fragrance of candles, became a cocoon of preparation. As Madeline adjusted the necklace, Genevieve's eyes met her reflection in the mirror – a portrait of elegance and anticipation.

With a final nod of approval, Madeline stepped back, allowing Genevieve to take in the full effect. She was pleased with how she looked, and ready to see what the night held for her.

The grand winter ball awaited, and she did not wish to be a moment late, so Genevieve descended the stairs of Ellsworth Manor. An intense excitement flooded her as she caught sight of the rest of her family, ready for the night ahead.

"Ah, you look lovely," her father told her, grinning proudly. "I am so glad that you are ready. The coach awaits."

There was a chill in the air, but Genevieve was not bothered by the cold. There was a heat flushing in her cheeks as she left the building and the family started on their journey to the ball. She kept her hands clutched tightly in her lap, trying to keep her intense anticipation hidden from everyone else. Although she was quite sure that she could hide anything from Harry. Her brother knew her all too well. Genevieve was quite sure that his eyes were upon her always.

Eventually, the family arrived at the village inn where the ball was being held, and a gasp escaped Genevieve's lips at the magical transformation that greeted her. The familiar inn, a cornerstone of village life, had undergone a stunning metamorphosis, now bathed in the enchantment of the grand winter ball. Candles flickered, casting a warm glow that danced across the snowy landscape outside. Icicles adorned the eaves, glistening like crystalline sculptures in the winter night. Festive decorations adorned every corner, turning the humble inn into a winter wonderland.

The air was filled with the sweet scent of pine, mingling with the warmth of the candles. The twinkling lights, strategically placed to create a celestial atmosphere, reflected in Genevieve's eyes as she took in the breathtaking scene. The village inn, familiar in its everyday charm, had become an ethereal haven of celebration and Genevieve struggled to contain herself. She had already been very excited about the night ahead, and now it truly felt like anything could happen.

The transformation extended beyond the decorations, which they soon discovered as they stepped inside the inn. The usual hum of village life was replaced by the melodies of a string quartet, their music weaving through the air with grace and elegance. Laughter echoed, and the dance floor, now a focal point of the festivity, beckoned guests to join the rhythmic celebration.

Genevieve marveled at the attention to detail — the shimmering table cloths, the delicate snowflakes hanging from the ceiling, and the radiant smiles of the villagers dressed in their finest attire. The grand winter ball unfolded before Genevieve like a dream. Her gaze swept across the room, taking in the flickering candles, the festive decorations, and the lively swirl of dancers on the floor. However, the moment her eyes settled on Lord Alastair Fitzroy, standing alongside Lady Isabella Cavendish, a sudden tightening in her stomach turned the joyous atmosphere into one of discomfort.

The memory of her last confrontation with Alastair echoed in her mind, including his displeased reaction to her rejection. The unease that had lingered since then intensified as Alastair's presence became a stark reality in the transformed inn. The air seemed to thicken with unresolved tension.

Genevieve could not shake the knot of nerves that twisted in her stomach. As she moved through the crowd, her eyes inadvertently met Alastair's, even if that was something she had been trying her hardest to avoid. His gaze, cool and composed, sent a painful shiver down her spine. It seemed like he wanted to approach her again tonight, and that was the last thing in the world that Genevieve wanted. She simply wished to avoid him as much as she could.

But it seemed like he did not seem to feel the same way.

Much to Genevieve's horror, it appeared that Alastair was making his way towards her through the crowd, with what looked like a terrible twinkle in his eye. Was he about to cause a scene here? Because no one would be pleased about that.

A mix of apprehension and discomfort tightened her stomach as he neared her. What on earth could he possibly want? Alastair's composed demeanor did little to ease the unease that surged within her. When he finally stood before her, a polite smile gracing his features, Genevieve felt a twinge of apprehension.

"Good evening, Lady Ellsworth," Alastair said, a polite smile playing on his lips. "How are you?"

Genevieve's mouth ran day. She was very worried about what was to come, and who was watching them. "I am fine, thank you, Lord Fitzroy, and how are you?"

He grinned ear to ear. "I am quite well. In fact, I wanted to ask you if you would do me the honour of sharing a dance with me?"

Genevieve hesitated as the question hung in the air, her eyes flickering to the expectant gazes of the surrounding guests. She forced a delicate smile, well aware of the societal expectations that bound her. "Lord Fitzroy, it would be my pleasure," she replied, accepting his invitation reluctantly.

He could probably sense that she was unhappy with this, but that did not stop him from extending his arm to take her. Genevieve had no choice but to take his hand. As they moved toward the dance floor, the lively music seemed to mock the turmoil in her mind. The steps of the dance, usually a joyous expression of shared celebration, now felt like a series of careful maneuvers in an intricate social dance.

As Alastair led her in the dance, Genevieve's eyes flitted across the room, catching glimpses of familiar faces. The ton, ever watchful and quick to speculate, observed the dance with keen interest. Their glances seemed to amplify the pressure on Genevieve, turning the dance into a public performance.

With each step, she wished for the dance to end swiftly, for the strains of the quartet to lead them to the conclusion of this forced engagement. The winter wonderland of the ballroom, which had initially captivated her, now felt like a gilded cage where societal expectations held sway.

"Have you been enjoying the winter time?" Alastair asked Genevieve pointedly, as if he expected her to converse with him while she danced. As if it were not enough that she was in his arms, which was the last place in the world she wanted to be.

"Oh, yes, thank you." Genevieve kept her tone as level as she could. "And you?"

"I have been having a *very* interesting time," he said with a low chuckle. "Very interesting indeed."

That was definitely a push for her to ask more, but Genevieve did not want to give him what he wanted. She did not wish to know how he had been spending his time. With a bit of luck, he had found another lady to propose to, one who was far more interested in him.

"I have been very interested in the history of the region," Alastair continued, undeterred by her lack of interest. The scent of alcohol on his breath reached her, making Genevieve's stomach churn. His words, usually filled with a veneer of courtesy, now seemed to slither through the air. "There appears to be a lot to be unraveled here, do you not think? Mysteries surround us all the time, and we must look into all of them."

What did that mean? What was Alastair getting at? He seemed to have a point of view here, one that he wished for her to understand, but one that she did not get. He could not possibly know about the mysteries of Graftonshire, not like she did. There was no way. How could he have heard too?

Unfortunately, she did not get a chance to ask. Not that she knew the right words to ask anyway. The dance finally came to a close, and Genevieve managed a polite curtsy, hiding the relief that washed over her. Alastair, too, offered a courteous bow, and they parted ways hopefully for the rest of the evening. Genevieve did not like the black cloud that Alastair threatened to bring to the night.

"Lady Ellsworth."

Another voice calling out to her made Genevieve smile. This was a voice that she wanted to hear, and a person she wanted to talk to. Instinctively, she turned around, and there he was — *Jonathan*, looking exceptionally handsome in a way that momentarily stole her breath.

His usual attire of crisp waist coats and tailored coats had transformed into a symphony of elegance. Jonathan stood before her in a deep midnight blue tail coat adorned with intricate silver embroidery that caught the ambient light. The tails of the coat flowed with each movement, adding a touch of drama to his silhouette. A pristine white cravat adorned his neck, a stark contrast to the richness of the coat.

Beneath the jacket, he wore a waist coat of a slightly lighter shade, a subtle nod to sophistication. The fabric shimmered in the soft glow of the chandeliers, and the delicate silver filigree buttons added a touch of regality. His trousers, impeccably tailored, completed the ensemble, tapering down to polished black dancing shoes that moved seamlessly across the polished floor.

A subtle flush of color adorned his cheeks as he extended his hand, a mix of confidence and genuine humility in his gaze. "May I have this dance, Genevieve?" he asked, his voice a melodic cadence that resonated with sincerity.

Genevieve could not help but be captivated. With a gracious smile, she placed her hand in his and nodded. "Of course."

The strains of the waltz enveloped Genevieve as she glided across the ballroom floor with Jonathan. The dance was a stark contrast to the formalities she had endured with Alastair. In Jonathan's arms, the atmosphere shifted, and an unexpected joy began to unfurl within her.

His hand on her waist felt both reassuring and electrifying, guiding her with a rhythm that resonated with her very heart beat. As they twirled and spun, the world around them seemed to blur, leaving only the enchantment of the moment. Jonathan's touch was a balm, dispelling the lingering discomfort from the previous dance.

She stole a glance at him, and a genuine smile graced her lips. Jonathan, resplendent in his midnight blue tail coat, exuded a quiet confidence that resonated with her. His eyes held a warmth that surpassed the polished surface of social decorum, and the sincere gentleness in his gaze stirred something within her — a connection that went beyond the dance floor. A connection that had been building from the very first moment she laid eyes on this man.

The contrast with Alastair was striking. Alastair's dance had been laden with societal expectations and veiled conversations that left her unsettled. In Jonathan's embrace, the weight of those expectations seemed to dissipate. She felt uplifted and excited by his presence, and a thrill coursed through her veins just to have him this close.

The final strains of the waltz melted away, leaving Genevieve and Jonathan standing together, caught in the echo of the dance's fading magic. Time had slipped through their fingers too swiftly, leaving a yearning for more. As their eyes met, she sensed an unspoken connection, a shared understanding that the dance had been an all too brief respite from the constraints of time and expectation.

Jonathan's gaze held a warmth that mirrored her own sentiments. "Genevieve," he said, his voice a gentle caress against the lingering notes of the music, "would you care to join me for a moment? There is something I would like to share with you."

A flutter of anticipation danced in her chest as she nodded in agreement. Together, they navigated the elegant maze of the ballroom, seeking refuge in a quiet corner where the ambient hum of the festivities gave way to a more intimate atmosphere.

The soft glow of a solitary candelabrum cast a warm embrace over their secluded space. Jonathan, his eyes earnest, invited her to share the cushioned alcove with him. The hushed conversations and laughter of the ballroom formed a distant backdrop as they settled into the quietude, a sanctuary for open and honest conversation.

"Genevieve," Jonathan began, his eyes filled with a mix of excitement and uncertainty, "I was wondering if you would like to continue our adventure?"

Her curiosity piqued, Genevieve met his gaze, waiting for the revelation that danced behind his earnest eyes. "At the River Lox? But we did not find anything last time…"

"I think we need to take a trip to Grafton Castle?" Jonathan's question hung in the air, unexpected and thrilling.

The mention of Grafton Castle stirred a flicker of intrigue within Genevieve. The castle, with its ancient corridors and hidden chambers, had always held an air of mystery. It was a place whispered about in tales and legends, a symbol of untold secrets waiting to be unraveled.

Jonathan continued, his voice laced with enthusiasm, "I have been perusing my uncle's journal, and I believe I have stumbled upon clues that might lead us to the heart of Grafton Castle. I think that is where we would have ended up in our journey anyway. This will save us some time… if I am correct."

"Yes, of course," she agreed, the words slipping from her lips like a whispered promise.

The ballroom's opulence faded as the evening wore on, and the constraints of societal norms reminded Genevieve of the boundaries that governed their interactions. Jonathan and she could not linger in quiet corners, exchanging whispers and confidences, without inviting the watchful eyes and hushed murmurs of onlookers.

As they parted ways for the night, Genevieve felt a twinge of reluctance. The prospect of being near Jonathan, of continuing the captivating conversations that had ignited a spark within her, beckoned like a distant melody. However, the constraints of propriety demanded they retreat from the shadows and return to the dance of expected formalities.

She sighed inwardly, understanding that the societal dance dictated their movements, even when her heart longed for an extended rendezvous with Jonathan. A subtle smile graced her lips as she navigated the ballroom, the polished floor echoing the cadence of her thoughts.

At least, she mused, there were plans for the morning — a visit to Grafton Castle with Jonathan. The anticipation of the upcoming adventure brought a glimmer of excitement to her eyes. Whether they would uncover hidden treasures or unravel the castle's mysteries remained uncertain, but the prospect of exploring alongside the duke warmed her heart.

As the ball continued in full swing, Genevieve found herself lost in the ebb and flow of the festivities. She engaged in polite conversation, danced with other partners, and maintained the facade of a lady immersed in the social whirl. Yet, beneath the surface, the promise of the next morning lingered like a secret, shared between Jonathan and her.

The moon light spilled through the ballroom's arched windows, casting a silvery glow over the scene. Genevieve stole glances across the room, catching glimpses of Jonathan engaged in conversation with other guests. The connection they shared remained unspoken in the public eye, a subtle dance of glances and smiles that hinted at the bond growing stronger with each passing moment.

As the night waned and the final notes of the orchestra's melody echoed, Genevieve bid her farewells to the remaining guests. The ballroom, once alive with laughter and music, transformed into a hushed sanctuary. In the solitude of her thoughts, she could not help but feel a sense of contentment — the promise of a morning rendezvous with Jonathan, an adventure awaiting in the shadowed corridors of Grafton Castle. The whispers of potential treasures may have been uncertain, but the warmth in her heart at the thought of being near the duke again was undeniable.

# CHAPTER 22

The morning light filtered through the frost laden window, casting delicate patterns on the glass. Jonathan's attention was momentarily drawn to the intricate designs, a fleeting distraction before his thoughts plunged back into the whirlwind of the previous night. The grand winter ball, with its enchanting atmosphere and lively dance, unfolded like a vivid tapestry in his mind.

The soft glow of Genevieve's face lingered in his memory, an image that refused to fade with the dawn. The echo of her laughter, a melodic interlude in the grand ballroom, resonated in his ears. Each twirl and step on the dance floor, the feel of her hand in his, continued to play on a loop in his mind — a captivating refrain that refused to be silenced by the morning light.

The warmth of Genevieve's presence, the subtle exchanges that transcended words, filled the room like a lingering fragrance. Jonathan could almost feel the soft texture of her gown, the warmth of the dance floor, and the gentle pressure of her hand in his. The morning light, though casting a new day, could not dispel the enchantment that still lingered in the recesses of his thoughts. He was so grateful that they had a chance to talk, and that today they would be adventuring again together. It absolutely thrilled him.

He smiled to himself, and slid his eyes closed for just a moment...

Unfortunately, closing his eyes took him back to a moment of his past he had been trying his hardest to forget. Even with Genevieve giving him other things to think about, he could not shake off the tragedy he had caused and endured. The ship remained in the peripheries of his mind, as did the biting cold, and the thrashing waves.

Would he ever be able to escape what had happened that tragic day?

As Jonathan grappled with the conflicting currents of his past and the burgeoning emotions stirred by Genevieve, a subtle realization dawned. Perhaps, in the midst of the storm, there was room for warmth, for connections that defied the cold grasp of history. The sea may have taken much from him, but it did not take the capacity for new beginnings, for the unexpected warmth that Genevieve's presence brought into his life.

He had been so determined to keep people at arm's length ever since that day, but he had not been expecting to meet anyone quite like Lady Genevieve Ellsworth. She had really changed things for him in ways he was not expecting, and it was something he did not know how to deal with.

Pushing the covers off, Jonathan rose from the bed and approached the window, his gaze fixed on the gentle snowfall outside. The tranquility of the scene stood in stark contrast to the storm brewing within his heart. Undeniable emotions for Genevieve tugged at the edges of his self imposed vow, and he found himself on the precipice of a decision.

The questions tormented his thoughts: Did Genevieve share the same depth of feeling? Could she look past the scars of his past and perceive the man he had become? The scars, both physical and emotional, had long served as a protective barrier, shielding him from the vulnerabilities of emotional entanglements. Yet, Genevieve's presence had breached those defenses, leaving him grappling with a sea of emotions he had carefully suppressed.

Standing by the window, Jonathan grappled with the conflicting currents of his heart, uncertain of the path ahead. The storm of uncertainty raged within, and the choice to confront the depths of his feelings for Genevieve loomed large — a choice that could either lead to newfound warmth or plunge him back into the familiar solitude he had long embraced.

\*\*\*

Later in the morning, as Jonathan approached the imposing structure of Grafton Castle with Genevieve and Harry in tow, the world seemed to pause in reverence. The castle, with its towering walls and silent corridors, stood as a testament to centuries gone by. The air was thick with the weight of history, and the hushed whispers of the wind seemed to carry echoes of tales long forgotten. It was exactly as his uncle had written about in his journal, which filled Jonathan with confidence. There was something here, he was sure of it.

He could not wait to prove to Genevieve and Harry that too.

As the three of them crossed the threshold in to the castle, the atmosphere shifted. The grandeur of the entrance hall, adorned with faded tapestries and aged portraits, hinted at the opulence that once graced these halls. The creaking floor boards beneath their feet seemed to resonate with the footsteps of those who had walked these corridors in ages past. Jonathan could only begin to imagine what lives had been lived here. The loves, the balls, the adventures. It had to have been a wonderful place once upon a time.

"What do we do?" Genevieve asked as she drank in the atmosphere surrounding them all. "Where do we begin? Do you know where to look? Did the journal say?"

Jonathan shook his head. "I am not too sure. I think we should explore the whole building."

Harry nodded in a determined agreement which made Jonathan smile. This could be a really fun day, there could be a lot to explore.

The endless rooms, each holding its secrets and mysteries, beckoned them further in to the heart of Grafton Castle. The air inside was cool and musty, a mixture of dust and history. The dim light filtering through grimy windows added an ethereal quality to the surroundings, casting long shadows that danced along the stone walls.

As they explored, Jonathan could not shake the feeling that the castle itself was a living entity, its stones imbued with the memories of bygone eras. The portraits on the walls, though faded with time, seemed to watch their every move with an almost spectral intensity. The silence that enveloped the castle was a canvas waiting to be painted with the stories of its past.

They ventured deeper, down winding corridors and up narrow staircases. Each room held a piece of the puzzle, a fragment of the castle's history waiting to be discovered. The air was thick with anticipation as they uncovered forgotten chambers and hidden alcoves, the very fabric of Grafton Castle unfolding before them like a tapestry of the past.

In the heart of the castle, they discovered a vast library, shelves lined with ancient tomes and dusty manuscripts. The scent of old parchment and leather filled the air, adding to the timeless aura of the room. As Jonathan ran his fingers over the spines of the books, he could not help but feel a connection to the scholars and historians who had once sought knowledge within these walls.

"What is this?" Harry asked, distracting Jonathan from studying the books. "It looks like there is a thin hallway here. Where could this lead?"

"The entrance is slightly concealed," Genevieve gasped in surprise. "That is suspicious. Something could be hidden here."

She looked at Jonathan as he approached them, with delight shining in her gaze. He was not sure if they had stumbled across something important here, but he hoped that they had. He did not want to be the one to dim the excitement in her gaze.

"Let us look," Jonathan declared as he turned sideways and slipped inside. There he found himself looking at a strange room, once hidden in the shadows of time, which revealed itself with a peculiar charm. Ancient carvings adorned the walls, telling stories of eras long past. Oddly placed bricks hinted at concealed passages, and the air held a mysterious weight, as if the room had witnessed secrets that transcended the pages of history. "I am not sure what is here, but I think you should come."

Genevieve followed him first, slightly covering her dress with dust as she did. But she did not seem to mind that she had gotten dirty. She was too interested in this new room. Harry followed, struggling slightly with his leg, but it did not take long for him to be impressed too. The intense anticipation built endlessly within Jonathan. He only hoped that this would lead to something positive. With a bit of luck, they would find the treasure here.

"Look at this," Jonathan murmured as he took a step deeper in to the room. "What is this?"

In the center of the room, an old map unfurled across a table, its edges yellowed with age. The lines on the map seemed to converge at a specific point, a destination waiting to be unveiled. The thrill of discovery sparked in Jonathan's chest, a flame that mirrored the curiosity in Genevieve and the watchful vigilance in Harry's eyes.

"Where do you think this is?" Genevieve asked as she joined Jonathan.

"It is Graftonshire," Harry gasped. "Look at the landmarks. This is a crucial piece of the puzzle. All the places we have visited on this treasure hunt are mapped out. Seabrook Ruins, the Moors, the River Lox..."

Before Harry could continue, a chilling wind blew through the room, extinguishing the lanterns that flickered with a dim glow. The room plunged into semi darkness, shadows dancing on the walls like silent observers of the unfolding drama.

In the muted light, a male figure emerged from the obscurity, his face a mask of anger and greed. The atmosphere shifted, becoming charged with tension, as if the very air crackled with the conflicting energies of their pursuits.

*Lord Alastair Fitzroy.*

What on earth was Alastair doing here? What was going on? Jonathan could not even begin to imagine how they had been found here by this person who seemed to have a visceral hatred for him, even if he did not know where it came from.

Jonathan felt a surge of unease. The discovery they were on the brink of unveiling now hung in the balance, overshadowed by Alastair's unexpected appearance. The once thriving excitement for uncovering Grafton Castle's secrets now gave way to a foreboding sense of conflict.

Alastair's eyes gleamed with an unsettling mix of determination and avarice. His sudden entrance, like an ominous gust of wind, disrupted the delicate equilibrium the trio had established in their quest for the castle's mysteries. As he advanced in to the dimly lit space, the silence between them grew heavy. The map, the carvings, and the secrets concealed in the castle's walls seemed to wait in anticipation, as if the very stones held their breath, uncertain of the outcome that would unfold.

Jonathan's hand instinctively tightened around the lantern, his gaze locking on to Alastair's.

"What are you doing here?" Jonathan asked, trying to suppress his anger as much as he could. "What is happening?"

He could not help but notice that Genevieve seemed to step behind him, as if she did not want to be in Alastair's view. She did not wish him to lay eyes upon her, which instantly brought out his protective side. If Genevieve did not like Alastair, then she would not be bothered by him.

"What am *I* doing here?" Alastair sneered. "I think you already know. I am here to stop you taking what does not belong to you."

"What..." Jonathan swallowed hard. "What are you talking about?"

Alastair's voice cut through the stale air of the ancient room like a bitter wind. "You think you can just waltz in here and claim the treasure for yourselves?" His eyes, ablaze with anger, darted accusingly between Jonathan, Genevieve, and Harry. "I will not allow that to happen."

Jonathan, standing tall and defiant, retorted, "We are not here to claim anything unlawfully. We are unraveling the mysteries, just like those who came before us."

Alastair scoffed, his disbelief palpable. "Mysteries? You are after the treasure, just like everyone else. And you," he pointed a finger at Jonathan, "you are not fooling anyone with your noble facade. I know your kind."

Genevieve, her patience wearing thin, stepped forward, revealing herself at long last. "This is about preserving history, not personal gain. We have dedicated ourselves to understanding the secrets this castle holds. We have been on a treasure hunt, and we are coming to the end of it..."

But Alastair was not swayed. "History? You are all blinded by the glitter of gold. I will not let you desecrate what rightfully belongs to Graftonshire. Did my warnings not stop you? I know you received my note at the River Lox. Why did you not follow it?"

"That was you?" Harry gasped out in horror. "Why would you do that to us?"

Alastair laughed nastily, confirming to Jonathan that he was right to have a bad feeling about this man. "To stop you from doing *this*."

Jonathan, maintaining his composure, countered, "We are not desecrating anything. We are here to unearth the truth, to honour the history that belongs to this land."

Alastair, unmoved, sneered. "Truth? You are playing a dangerous game, and you are going to regret it."

The argument, a clash of ideals and intentions, resonated through the ancient room, leaving an indelible mark on the pursuit of Grafton Castle's secrets. The lanterns flickered in the dim light, casting erratic shadows on the carvings and maps that adorned the walls. The air, thick with unresolved conflict, hung heavy with the realization that the hunt for the treasure was far from over.

# CHAPTER 23

Genevieve's surroundings in Grafton Castle felt alive with an ancient energy, as though the very stones were witnesses to the unfolding drama. The room pulsed with a silent tension that seemed to seep from the weathered walls, bearing the weight of centuries of untold stories and concealed treasures.

The intensity of the clash between Jonathan and Alastair sent a shiver down Genevieve's spine. The air crackled with the echoes of their words, and the stone walls seemed to absorb every nuance of the escalating conflict. Her breath quickened, matching the rhythm of her racing heart.

"How do I know it is not you who wishes to claim the treasure for your own?" Jonathan shot back, refusing to bend to Alastair's accusations.

"Because you did not overhear me talking about being rich. I heard you saying that."

Guilt flowed through Genevieve. That was a conversation she had between Jonathan and herself, but it was a playful one. They had not been serious, but it seemed like Alastair had overheard and misconstrued everything. How could Genevieve make this right now when Alistair was full of rage and not listening to anyone?

Beside her, Harry shifted, his protective instincts evident in the narrowing of his eyes and the tension in his posture. Genevieve could sense his readiness, the unspoken pledge to leap in and defend her, to end the confrontation before it spiraled any further. The weight of his loyalty felt like a reassuring anchor in the midst of the escalating tension. Her brother had always been there for her no matter what had happened. Even if she did not always feel like she deserved it.

In that charged moment, Genevieve leaned subtly toward Harry, seeking solace in the unspoken connection. His steady gaze met hers, conveying not just protection but a shared determination to navigate the storm together. That was enough to give Genevieve the necessary courage to act.

Determined to mediate before this got even more out of hand than it already was, Genevieve's voice quivered as she stepped forward. "Please, enough!" she implored, her words carrying the weight of desperation, an attempt to be the voice of reason in this whirl wind of emotion. Her gaze shifted between Jonathan and Alastair, each plea punctuating the growing tension in the room. "We do not need to argue about this. There have been some miscommunications here, which we can easily rectify by just talking."

As she moved to stand between the two men, seeking a semblance of peace, the castle's age old floor betrayed her. The splintering sound of wood reached her ears, and before she could process it, the ground beneath her gave way. In a heartbeat, she found herself plummeting downwards, the air rushing past her, and her fingers desperately scrambling for purchase on the edge. A cry flew out of her mouth, but she could not hear any sounds.

The world seemed to blur as Genevieve fought against the force of gravity. Panic surged through her, and the echoes of the argument above faded into the background. In those fleeting moments of descent, her mind raced, and the realization of the precarious situation enveloped her in a chilling embrace.

Her fingers grazed the edge of the floor, desperately clutching at the hope of halting the fall. The cold stone slipped through her grasp, and fear gripped her heart as she continued to descend into the unknown depths below Grafton Castle. The echoes of the argument above became distant whispers, and the shadows of the past seemed to reach out to claim her in the darkness.

Her heart pounded fiercely, the world narrowing down to the yawning chasm below and the frantic echoes of Harry's panicked shouts. Genevieve felt his desperate attempts to reach her, the urgency in his movements evident even in the chaos. The cold air rushed past her, and the dim light from above seemed to fade as the depth of the chasm became more profound. Genevieve braced herself for the impact. The cold stone rushed up to meet her, and in that suspended moment, time seemed to stretch. The echoes of the argument, the urgent shouts, and the struggle above merged into a symphony of chaos, a cacophony that accompanied her descent into the unknown.

*What just happened?* She wondered in shock. *I can not believe that... this castle is puzzling.*

Time unfurled in unpredictable patterns while Genevieve tried to steady herself in the deep darkness, bending and contorting in ways that seemed to defy the constraints of reality. Each moment stretched infinitely, echoing with the weight of anticipation and uncertainty. In the midst of this temporal dance, a pivotal realization emerged — one that etched itself in to the fabric of Genevieve's memory.

*Jonathan.* It was thoughts of him that kept her feeling safe and warm, even in a place she was not sure about. She cared about him, she liked him... over time she was starting to think that she might have even come to love him.

She never expected to fall in love. She thought that she had closed her heart off to everyone, she did not think of herself as a person worthy of love ever since Harry had his accident, but that had not stopped her from falling. Despite herself, her heart had opened up to this man, and now she was not sure what to do about that. Especially not when she was in a hole that she was not sure she could climb out of any time soon.

"Genevieve, I am here." Jonathan's voice broke through the silence, which helped her relax a little. "Take my hand."

The air crackled with an electric tension as he seized a desperate, defining moment. His hand, a life line woven with determination, closed around hers. In that instant, the world held its breath, and Genevieve's heart raced in tandem with the rhythm of time itself. The connection was more than physical; it was a bridge forged from the crucible of shared trials. Jonathan's grip, firm and unyielding, transcended the limits of mere touch. It spoke of a promise, a pact made in the crucible of adversity. As his fingers entwined with hers, a surge of strength coursed through Genevieve, leaving her momentarily breathless.

With a single, decisive pull, Jonathan wrenched her from the clutches of impending danger. The world blurred in motion, a kaleidoscope of fleeting images, but amid the chaos, their faces drew impossibly close. Inches apart, their breaths mingled, a silent testament to the shared ordeal that had brought them to this precipice.

"Are you alright?" Jonathan whispered as their eyes connected.

"Yes," she replied just as quietly with a small nod. "I think so."

Genevieve found herself caught in the gravity of Jonathan's gaze, a gravity that went beyond the immediate peril they faced. It was a gravity born of shared struggle, an unspoken alliance formed in the crucible of adversity. The world, once teetering on the edge of chaos, stabilized in the wake of their reunion.

As the echoes of their shared ordeal lingered, Jonathan's hand remained a steadfast anchor. The world outside this cocoon of shared relief might still be fraught with challenges, but in this suspended moment, Jonathan's grip promised a sanctuary — a sanctuary forged through strength, determination, and the unbreakable bond they had discovered in the crucible of chaos.

The echo of their shared relief was abruptly shattered by the ominous thunder of foot steps, resonating through the room like a harbinger of intrusion. Startled, Genevieve turned her gaze away from Jonathan, still grappling with the after shocks of her fall.

Alastair and Harry clearly had no idea who the footsteps belonged to either, which only made this even more confusing. What strange things were they about to encounter in this castle now?

"Here, I told you, I heard a commotion inside." A servant of the castle emerged from the shadows. The sounds of the argument had reached the outskirts of the castle, where the servant, with the faithful company of a dog cart, had been stationed. Sensing the disturbance, he acted swiftly, alerting the local authorities to the commotion within. "There is trouble."

The constables which followed the servants, their expressions a mix of curiosity and duty, surveyed the scene. Genevieve found herself caught between the tendrils of relief and the encroaching shadows of authority. She did not know who would get in trouble here, and she was afraid. If they truly were not supposed to be in the castle, searching for the treasure, then they could all end up with problems here.

"This is the man," the servant continued, thankfully pointing towards Alastair. "He is the one who came and caused trouble."

"I am not. I am merely here to put right a wrong..."

The vast room reverberated with the echoes of Alastair's protests, wild eyed and defeated as he was restrained by the authorities. Nothing he said seemed to change their minds at all. They were listening to the servant, thank goodness.

Alastair's once imposing figure now appeared diminished, the shadows of defeat etched across his features as he was removed from the room. The authorities, efficient and stern faced, took control of the situation, determined to take him away from there, to make him pay for what he had done.

However, amidst the controlled chaos, Genevieve's attention remained singularly focused on Jonathan. She could not even hear the words falling out of Alastair's mouth now, because she was only focused on *him*. Their eyes met, a silent exchange that surpassed the surrounding commotion. The shared ordeal, the brush with danger, had woven an invisible thread between them — one that neither could deny or escape.

Jonathan stood beside her, a pillar of strength amidst the upheaval. His presence offered a silent reassurance, a tangible anchor in the storm. The unspoken acknowledgment of their shared feelings hung in the air, a revelation spurred by the intensity of the recent events. The veil of denial, once carefully draped over unspoken emotions, had been lifted.

In the aftermath of the confrontation, as the authorities worked to restore order, Genevieve and Jonathan existed in a moment suspended in time. The air crackled with unspoken words, emotions too potent to be confined to the constraints of language. She did not know what was about to come next, but she could not contain her excitement. Everything felt like it was all going to be positive from here on out.

# CHAPTER 24

The musty air within the castle hung heavy with the aftermath of the confrontation with Alastair. Jonathan felt the weight of the recent events pressing down on him, each passing moment carrying the echoes of a tumultuous encounter. The castle, once a bastion of stability, now bore witness to the ripples of conflict and he was not sure how the place would recover. All the trials and tribulations he imagined occurring within the walls of this castle, he did not envision a row just like that one.

His chest rose and fell rapidly, the cadence of his breaths a demonstration to the lingering effects of adrenaline. The intensity of the confrontation still pulsed through his veins, leaving him on the precipice between the immediacy of action and the lingering of what had happened afterwards. The air itself seemed charged with the residue of tension, a palpable reminder of the recent struggle.

"You killed him!" Alastair cried out as he was tugged from the room by the police. "You are no duke, Jonathan. You are a failed ship captain who killed my friend, Trevor."

Jonathan's blood ran ice cold. He whipped his eyes away from Genevieve to stare at Alastair, to see what he was talking about. How did Alastair know anything about his failed ship voyage, when most people knew nothing? He was not even thinking about Genevieve in this moment, and how she must be feeling about this news. All he could focus on was *him*.

"You were at the helm of the ship, Jonathan, and you allowed us all to struggle in the storm. You allowed members of your crew to die."

Now Jonathan knew where he recognized this man from, and it was a chilling revelation.

The specter of Alastair's accusations loomed large in the recesses of Jonathan's mind. They had been on the same voyage, traversing the unpredictable seas that etched stories on the faces of sailors. The blame, heavy and unwarranted, had settled squarely on Jonathan's shoulders. Alastair was right. He truly was at fault. His mouth hung open, because there was no response he could give to Alastair. There was nothing he could say as the man was dragged away from the room, to hopefully be locked up.

Alastair might be gone, but the accusations remained.

"What was that about?" Harry asked, his voice heavy with worry. "I did not know you were a ship captain."

Jonathan glanced over to Genevieve, who was staring at him wide eyed with the same questions playing on her lips. He knew it was time to be open and honest with the two people who he had spent the winter with, even if he was not ready for it.

"I was once a Navy captain," he said with his eyes on the floor. There was no way he could look at anyone as he finally said this. He was going to have to revert back to the area of his past he no longer wanted to recall. "And there was a day when the weather was not great, but I did not believe that there would be a storm. I assumed that my very talented crew would be able to handle it. A decision which I have regretted ever since, because the storm was far worse than I ever could have imagined." His head fell in to his hands, as his heart broke a little more. "People did die. It was a terrible day for us all."

Much to his surprise, Jonathan felt the softness of someone touching his arm, comforting him as he spoke of the worst day of his life. He lifted his eyes up just a little to see Genevieve holding on to him. His heart almost skipped a beat because he did not know what this meant.

"Accidents can torture us in ways we never expect," she told him seriously. "I have also been holding onto guilt, for what happened to my brother…"

"Why?" Harry interjected. "What happened to me was a mere accident, not your fault."

Tears filled Genevieve's eyes. "I called out to you, Harry…"

"Yes, trying to warn me," Harry agreed. "And I was too young and too slow to react on time. Anything that happened to me is not your fault." Then Harry turned his attention to Jonathan. "And what happened to you is the same. An accident. You can not be blamed for the storm."

Jonathan smiled thinly. "But it is my fault we headed out in to the ocean in that weather."

Harry furrowed his brows in confusion. "But you did not do it on purpose, am I right? You did not head out to the water in the hope that people would die."

"Of course not!" Jonathan pressed his hand to his chest in shock. "I would never want anyone to die."

"Exactly, so you can not hold all the blame on yourself. The same goes for you Genevieve. I do not wish for you to blame yourself either. Just because I sometimes have trouble with my leg, does not mean it has impacted me so terribly that I blame you."

Jonathan and Genevieve looked at one another, and for the first time in his whole life, he felt truly *seen*. He was not the only one who had held onto guilt for as long as he could remember. Genevieve also held onto something from her past that she blamed herself for. He reached out and held her hands, grateful for this level of connection he had never experienced with another person before. The feelings that had been slowly blooming up within him, grew even more and almost exploded.

Everything else melted away into nothingness. A smile spread across Jonathan's lips. This was the happiest he had felt in a very long time. The weight of what had happened on that ship still pressed down on him, but it was nowhere near as heavy as it had been before. Just talking about his past to someone who understood him was wonderful.

Perhaps he did not need to be unhappy forever.

"Wait, what is this?" Just as Jonathan was about to get lost in the moment in Genevieve's eyes, and maybe even confess how he was feeling, Harry interjected once more. "Look, Genevieve. The hole in which you fell, there seems to be something inside."

Curiosity got the best of Genevieve and she pulled away. Jonathan eagerly followed as the memory of the treasure hunt flooded him once more. He had been distracted by Alastair and the memories of his ship voyage, but Harry had just reminded him that they came here for a reason, and he could not wait to see if that was all about to be worth it.

"It is a chest," Genevieve gushed out, the excitement lacing her tone as she flashed her happy eyes at Harry and Jonathan. "Do you think this is *the* treasure?"

Jonathan was not sure what to say. In the hole, the ornate treasure chest, a relic of a bygone era, stood before Jonathan like a sentinel of secrets waiting to be unveiled. The promise of history, intricately woven into the chest's ornate design, echoed through the chamber. He wanted to tell Genevieve that of course this was the chest that they had been searching for, but until he knew for certain, he could not say a word.

As he knelt before the chest, Jonathan felt the weight of generations pressing upon him. The anticipation, a tangible force in the air, seemed to bridge the gap between the past and the present. The castle, with its ancient stones and whispered tales, bore witness to the unfolding of a legacy waiting to be unearthed.

"I will look now," he said quietly, as if he were worried about being disrupted once more. But no footsteps came, no yelling broke through the atmosphere. It was time.

His fingers traced the intricate patterns adorning the chest as he carefully unlatched it. The metal clasps yielded with a soft, deliberate creak, as if acknowledging the significance of the moment. The lid, once sealed by the passage of time, now revealed itself to the eager seeker.

"Oh my goodness," Genevieve called out in excitement. "This truly looks like treasure."

"I can not believe we have found it," Harry agreed.

As the chest opened, a breath caught in Jonathan's throat. The contents, hidden from the world for generations, lay before him — a testament to the stories woven into the fabric of Grafton Castle. The treasures within spoke of lives lived, challenges overcome, and the passage of time marked by moments of both triumph and tragedy.

"It is true," he called out excitedly. "This is exactly what we have been looking for."

His uncle's words written in the journal came to life in front of him. The map was all correct. Everything that they had been hunting for was right here in front of him.

In the flickering light of the chamber, the artifacts within the chest seemed to come alive. Each piece held a story, a fragment of a narrative waiting to be shared. The air itself hummed with the resonance of history, an echo of the lives that had left their mark on Grafton Castle.

"There are gold coins," Genevieve said excitedly.

"Jewelery as well. This is wonderful," Harry laughed. "Who would have thought that Graftonshire would have so much."

But Jonathan's eyes were fixed on something else. Among the artifacts, an exquisite ruby heart necklace immediately captured his attention. The deep red glow of the gem seemed to pulse with life, casting a warm aura that contrasted with the cool stone surroundings. The intricacies of its design spoke volumes, a testament to the craftsmanship of yesteryear.

As he lifted the necklace from its resting place, the metal links cool against his finger tips, Jonathan marveled at the artistry that had gone into its creation. The ruby heart seemed to hold within it the passion and stories of those who had once adorned it. Its presence added a touch of elegance to the dimly lit chamber, a beacon of time's enduring beauty.

Beneath the radiant center piece, a trove of treasures revealed itself. More gold coins, these bearing the stoic faces of long gone monarchs, whispered of a bygone era where kingdoms rose and fell. Rare manuscripts, with their delicate pages and weathered bindings, hinted at tales of old that had transcended the passage of time.

"What are these documents?" Genevieve asked as she picked some of the paper up carefully. "They look very interesting."

But again, Jonathan's eyes were drawn elsewhere. To him, among this captivating array, one item stood out — a parchment, its edges yellowed with age but its significance undiminished. Jonathan carefully unfolded the fragile paper, his eyes tracing the faded ink of carefully penned words. The parchment seemed to cradle a story, a narrative waiting to be unfurled in the quiet chamber.

*My Dearest Isabella,*

*As the ink flows on to this parchment, I am acutely aware of the distances that separate us. These words are but feeble messengers carrying the weight of my heart's deepest yearnings. In the silent corridors of Grafton Castle, I find myself haunted by the echo of your laughter, the gentle rustle of your skirts, and the warmth of your touch.*

*The necklace, with its ruby heart, stands before me — a silent witness to our undying affection. It was your most cherished possession, a token of the love that knows no bounds. When the world deemed our connection forbidden, it was this emblem of our bond that gave us solace in the secrecy of our stolen moments.*

*The ruby heart, with its deep red glow, symbolized the fire that burned within us. Each glance, each stolen kiss, spoke of a love that defied the rigid expectations of our station. It was the tether that bound our souls in a dance of passion, a secret flame that illuminated the shadows of my home.*

*But, my love, circumstances have conspired against us. The walls of duty and expectation have closed in, forcing us to part ways. The necklace, once adorning your graceful neck, now lies dormant, its glow a testament to the love that still resides within its delicate links.*

*As I pen these words, I am tormented by the knowledge that our paths may never cross again in this life time. The ache in my heart is mirrored in the silent chambers of Grafton Castle, where the shadows of our love linger like ghosts of a time that once was.*

*Remember me, my dearest, as I shall remember you. Let the ruby heart be a beacon of our love, a flame that refuses to be extinguished by the passage of time. In the quiet solitude of these stone walls, know that you are not forgotten, and our love remains etched in the annals of Graftonshire's history.*

*Yours, now and always,*
*The Duke*

"Oh wow." Jonathan was stunned by what he was reading. He was blown away. The words on the parchment danced across the page, revealing a tale of love and loss, heart breaking loss. It was a window into the lives of those who had once called Grafton Castle home. As Jonathan immersed himself in the narrative, he felt a connection to the past that transcended the physical artifacts around him. "This letter... it is..."

He did not have the words. Instead, he lost himself in the words once more, reading them again. The aged parchment, fragile and yellowed, unfolded in Jonathan's hands like a whisper from the past. The elegant script, written with a quill that had long since turned to dust, revealed the poignant words penned by a Duke of Graftonshire to his lost love.

The ruby necklace mentioned in the letter, now cradled in his palm, took on new significance as the tale unfolded. It had been the lost love's most cherished possession, a symbol of the undying affection between the Duke and his beloved. The ruby heart, with its deep red glow, had once adorned the neck of a woman whose presence lingered in the corners of Grafton Castle like a phantom of the past.

However, as Jonathan reflected on the journey that had brought them here — the danger they faced, the shared glances with Genevieve, the silent understanding between them — he realized that something profound had crystallized within him. The value of these artifacts, while undeniable, could not compare to the intangible wealth of emotions that had blossomed amid the chaos.

As he stood in the midst of Grafton Castle's treasures, Jonathan couldn't escape the weight of this realization. The necklace, once a symbol of a Duke's lost love, now resonated with new meaning — a reflection of the emotions swirling within his own heart. The wealth of history surrounding him faded into the background as the richness of their shared journey took center stage.

Summoning a courage he did not know he possessed, Jonathan rose from his kneeling position, the necklace cradled in his hands. The gleaming ruby heart captured the light, casting a warm hue across his features as he approached Genevieve. The moment hung in the air, pregnant with the weight of unspoken revelations.

Standing before her, he met her gaze, his eyes conveying a depth of emotion that transcended the artifacts around them. In that vulnerable moment, he said:

"Genevieve, I have just found the story about this chest, and this special necklace here."

"There is?" she asked with a sweet smile playing on her lips. "That is very exciting. I would love to hear it."

"Many years ago, the Duke of Grafton fell deeply in love with a woman named Isabella. Their love blossomed amidst the grandeur of this very castle. In a gesture of his affection, the duke commissioned a magnificent ruby necklace for Isabella, a piece of unparalleled beauty." He could see Genevieve's eyes fluttering with excitement. "This necklace, adorned with the most exquisite rubies, became a symbol of their love. However, fate had its own designs. A series of unforeseen events separated the duke and Isabella, and the necklace, once a token of love, became a bitter sweet reminder of what was lost."

"Oh my." Genevieve saddened. "That is so terribly tragic. Love is so rare in life. What a shame that they could not explore that love."

Those words gave Jonathan the courage to do what he never thought he would. It allowed him to speak his vulnerable feelings. The ones he never expected to feel, but now he knew life truly was too short to ignore this love. He did not want to live a life without being happy. Maybe he had made some mistakes in his life, and those mistakes had led to tragedy, but Genevieve had also made mistakes. She had also harmed someone else with her actions, but he knew that she deserved joy.

Perhaps it was time for him to start offering himself some grace as well.

He hesitated, feeling the weight of his words like a stone in his chest. Taking another deep breath, Jonathan summoned the courage to finally articulate the revelation that had blossomed within him. In a voice that carried both vulnerability and sincerity, he uttered the words that had echoed silently in the corridors of his heart.

"Genevieve, I need you to know that this winter time has been the best of my entire life. I have never been so happy and joyful. This treasure hunt has meant so much more to me than you could ever imagine. Throughout this time that we have spent together, I have undoubtedly fallen in love with you."

For a suspended moment, time seemed to freeze in the ancient castle chambers. The weight of his confession lingered in the air, a palpable gravity that held the space between them. The ambient light cast a glow on Genevieve's features, her eyes reflecting the mixture of surprise, curiosity, and perhaps something more.

# CHAPTER 25

As Jonathan's confession echoed through the ancient chambers of Grafton Castle, Genevieve felt her heart skip a beat. The words, sentiments she had secretly longed for but never quite dared to anticipate, hung in the air like a delicate melody. Emotions surged within her — a symphony of elation, surprise, and a whisper of apprehension, each note playing in harmony with the next.

In the chamber's muted light, their gazes met, and what she saw in Jonathan's eyes caught her off guard: raw vulnerability. It was as if he had unraveled the layers of his being, stripped away his defenses, and laid bare the intricate tapestry of his emotions. The scars of his past, the aspirations for what lay ahead, all exposed in the gentle glow of the ambient light.

A myriad of emotions played across Genevieve's features as she absorbed the weight of his words. Elation danced in her eyes, reflecting the joy of hearing the sentiments she had only dared to dream of. Surprise lingered, a delightful realization that this shared adventure had forged a connection deeper than she had imagined.

Yet, there was also a whisper of apprehension — a recognition that the revelation marked a pivotal moment in their journey. The ancient stones around them seemed to absorb the intensity of the emotions, each heartbeat echoing in the hallowed halls of Grafton Castle.

Jonathan's vulnerability held her captive, and for a brief moment, time seemed to stand still. In the exchange of gazes, a silent understanding passed between them, transcending spoken words. The muted light painted their faces with a soft glow, emphasizing the contours of vulnerability etched across Jonathan's features.

Grasping for the right words, she felt the weight of the moment settle upon her shoulders. The ambient light bathed them both in a muted glow as she softly admitted, "Jonathan, since our paths first crossed, I have felt a bond — a connection that defies explanation." Taking a measured breath, her voice quivered with the rawness of her emotions. The castle seemed to hold its breath in anticipation as she continued, "And now, in the quiet chambers of Grafton, amidst the echoes of the past and the warmth of this shared journey, I have come to realise... I have fallen in love with you also. This winter has also been the best time of my life."

The admission lingered in the air, each word carrying the weight of vulnerability and truth. In that moment, Genevieve felt a profound sense of liberation — the acknowledgment of her feelings, the unveiling of a sentiment she had held close to her heart. The ancient stones, the artifacts, and the timeless tales whispered their silent approval, as if the castle itself bore witness to the blossoming of a love story within its storied walls.

She never expected to fall in love with the handsome, mysterious duke, and to have him love her too, but it felt wonderful to have that happen. To have everything that she ever wanted happen, right at the end of her treasure hunt.

The profound silence hanging in the air lingered between them, cradling the echoes of their shared confessions within the ancient chambers of Grafton Castle. In the quietude, Jonathan's gaze held Genevieve's, a silent understanding passing between them like an unspoken promise. As if guided by an invisible force, he took a step forward, his movements deliberate and filled with purpose.

In his hands, Jonathan gently cradled the ruby heart necklace — the emblem of a by gone love story that now found itself intricately entwined with their own narrative. The delicate glow of the gem echoed the warmth of the ambient light, casting a soft illumination on the chamber's ancient stones.

With the utmost care, he fastened the necklace around Genevieve's neck. His fingers moved with a tenderness that spoke of reverence, as if sealing a pact between their hearts. The cool ruby pendant, once a silent witness to the Duke's poignant narrative, now found a new home against Genevieve's collarbone.

As the necklace settled into place, Genevieve felt the weight of its significance. The ruby heart, a symbol of enduring love, rested against her skin like a secret whispered through the ages. In that moment, their destinies became intertwined, the echoes of the past merging seamlessly with the present. She vowed to herself that she would do this necklace justice, she would ensure that her love story did not end with a tragic separation. Now that she had the duke in her life, and he had confessed how he felt about her, she would never let him go.

Jonathan's touch lingered for a heartbeat longer, a connection maintained through the delicate chain that now adorned her, making Genevieve's heart race. Genevieve traced the outline of the ruby heart with her finger tips, feeling the coolness of the gem against her skin. The chamber, once silent, now hummed with the resonance of their intertwined destinies. The necklace, a silent guardian of love's endurance, seemed to pulse with the heartbeat of their shared narrative.

In the muted light, Jonathan and Genevieve stood entwined, the ruby heart necklace a bridge between past and present. The castle's hallowed halls seemed to exhale, as if acknowledging the seamless fusion of their individual stories into a tapestry that now adorned both their hearts. The necklace, once a relic of the Duke's lost love, had become a talisman for a love story yet to be fully written — one that unfolded within the ancient stones of Grafton Castle, where the past and present danced in delicate harmony.

An invisible magnetism seemed to draw Jonathan and Genevieve closer, an irresistible force guiding their steps within the ancient chambers of Grafton Castle. The ambient light created a soft halo around them, casting a warm glow on their intertwined destinies. Jonathan's gaze held Genevieve's, a silent agreement passing between them like a shared secret.

With every heartbeat, the distance between them closed, and their faces drew nearer. The air seemed to hum with the energy of anticipation — a symphony of emotions playing beneath the surface. The echoes of shared confessions lingered, creating a delicate tension that only intensified the connection between their hearts.

In the quietude of the chamber, their lips met in a gentle, heartfelt kiss. It was a union of souls, a moment suspended in time. The world outside the castle walls ceased to exist as their emotions wove together in a tender embrace.

Jonathan's lips against hers were a whisper of understanding, a promise echoed in the quiet exchanges of their journey. The kiss, a delicate communion, spoke of vulnerability, courage, and the unspoken yearning that had led them to this sacred moment.

As their lips parted, the echo of the kiss lingered in the air. In that fleeting moment, Jonathan and Genevieve stood entwined, their hearts synchronized in the symphony of their shared journey. The kiss, a punctuation mark in the narrative of their story, marked the beginning of a new chapter. The start of the rest of their lives.

"Genevieve," Jonathan began, his voice filled with genuine emotion, resonated through the chamber like a melody. "Will you be my partner in this grand adventure called life? Will you walk beside me, face the challenges, and share in the triumphs?"

"What are you asking me?" Genevieve replied with a light chuckle. She already knew, but she wanted to hear him say it.

"I would like to know if you would marry me, Lady Ellsworth."

In that instant, time seemed to stretch, allowing the significance of the proposal to sink in. Genevieve met Jonathan's gaze, her heart echoing the fluttering wings of a butterfly in flight.

"Of course I will," she replied. Genevieve's heart, having weathered the storms of revelations and kisses, soared to new heights as Jonathan, with the utmost respect and tenderness, took her gloved hand in his. "I would like nothing more than to be your wife."

As their words hung in the air, a surge of elation filled Genevieve. The castle seemed to echo her joy, the ancient stones absorbing the warmth of their commitment. However, the elation deepened even further when the notion of seeking her father's blessing surfaced.

In a moment of serendipity, a delighted Harry stepped forward, having witnessed their profound exchange. His eyes sparkled with joy and approval, as he happily endorsed the love that had blossomed between Jonathan and Genevieve. The trio, standing amidst the echoes of Grafton Castle, formed a tableau of shared happiness — a symphony of joy that resonated through the chamber.

"You two are going to make one another very happy," Harry said with a soft smile playing on his lips. He had warned Genevieve many times that spending so much time with the duke might lead to rumors and gossip, but it was clear that he was no longer worried about a thing. Everything had worked out. "I am very happy to witness this proposal and for you two to start on your journey together. That ruby necklace is a wonderful symbol of all that is to come."

Genevieve's heart raced a lot faster as she envisioned what was coming next for her. She imagined nights spent by their home's roaring fireplace, their laughter mingling with the crackling flames. They would dance in the moonlit courtyard, creating new memories to weave into the fabric of their lives. Together, they would navigate the intricacies of life, facing challenges with resilience and celebrating triumphs with shared joy. Genevieve envisioned a future where the echoes of the Duke of Grafton's long lost love were replaced by the harmonies of their own enduring affection.

# EPILOGUE

*A month later...*

The air in Graftonshire chapel was infused with an atmosphere of anticipation, carrying the sweet fragrance of blooming flowers that adorned the intimate space. The stone walls, weathered by the ages, stood as silent witnesses to countless vows exchanged within their hallowed embrace. Stained glass windows filtered the warm sun light, casting a kaleidoscope of colors that danced across the pews and floor.

Jonathan, resplendent in a tailored suit, stood at the altar, his eyes reflecting a mixture of nerves and overwhelming joy. His gaze was fixed on the chapel's entrance, where the aisle awaited the entrance of his soon to be bride.

Genevieve, radiant in a gown that seemed to capture the essence of a thousand dreams, entered the chapel escorted by her father. Her dress was a vision of timeless elegance, befitting the grandeur of the occasion. The gown was a symphony of ivory silk, cascading in a gentle A line silhouette that accentuated her slender figure. The fabric embraced her curves before flowing gracefully into a sweeping train that trailed behind her like a cascade of moon lit silk.

The bodice was adorned with delicate lace. The intricate lace patterns formed an ethereal overlay, creating an illusion of blossoming vines that caressed the gown's silhouette. The neckline, a subtle sweet heart cut, added a touch of romance to the ensemble, framing Genevieve's collarbone with understated sophistication.

The gown's long, sheer sleeves showcased the same delicate lacework, extending down to her wrists in a subtle embrace. Each movement sent ripples through the sheer fabric, creating an enchanting play of light and shadow. A thin satin belt, adorned with subtle beading, cinched at Genevieve's waist, accentuating the gown's timeless silhouette and adding a hint of sparkle. The belt seamlessly transitioned into a cascade of silk covered buttons that trailed down the back of the dress, adding a touch of classic charm.

As Genevieve walked down the aisle, the gown seemed to capture the essence of a fairytale. The train, elegantly pooled at her feet, glided behind her, leaving a trail of whispers in its wake. The ivory silk seemed to glow in the soft light of the ceremony, and every step Genevieve took was a dance of grace and anticipation.

Completing the ensemble was a cathedral length veil, crafted from the finest tulle and delicately edged with matching lace. The veil framed Genevieve's face, adding a touch of ethereal beauty as did the ruby necklace sitting around her neck.

The soft strains of a piano played a melody that echoed through the sacred space as she walked. The hushed whispers of friends and family in attendance filled the air, creating a symphony of excitement that reverberated within the chapel's stone walls.

The chapel itself was adorned with simple yet elegant decorations. Bouquets of flowers adorned the ends of each pew, and delicate fairy lights adorned the archway leading to the altar, casting a warm and enchanting glow. The chapel's history seemed to come alive, its ageless beauty a perfect backdrop for the union about to unfold.

As Genevieve and her father approached the altar, Jonathan's eyes met hers, and the world outside the chapel seemed to fade into the background. The couple stood together, surrounded by an intimate gathering of friends and family, their love radiating like a beacon in the sacred space.

In the tender embrace of Graftonshire chapel, Jonathan and Genevieve stood at the altar, their hearts pulsating with the promise of forever. The soft glow of candles flickered around them, casting an ethereal light on the momentous occasion. As the wedding officiant started with the traditional wedding speech, the happiness flowed passionately between them. Neither of them knew that they could fall in love like this, and both of them wanted to make the most of these feelings forever.

Soon, it was time for them to express themselves, and Jonathan eagerly spoke first. His gaze unwavering, he began, "Genevieve, from the moment our paths converged, I knew that my heart had found its true home. Today, in the presence of our loved ones and the timeless stones of this chapel, I pledge my love to you. I promise to stand by you in joy and in sorrow, to cherish and support you in every endeavour. With you, I have discovered a love that transcends the ordinary — a love that is deep, enduring, and unyielding. Today, I willingly and eagerly choose you as my partner, my confidante, and my love for all the days of our lives."

Genevieve, in turn, spoke her vows with a voice that resonated with sincerity and passion. The words, carefully chosen and spoken from the depths of her heart, painted a portrait of a love that surpassed the boundaries of time. "Jonathan, in your presence, I have found a love that is as boundless as the sky and as steady as the earth beneath our feet. Today, surrounded by the echoes of this chapel and the warmth of our dear ones, I make these vows to you. I promise to be your confidante, your partner in adventure, and to love you unconditionally. I promise to stand with you through the highs and the lows, to share in your dreams and aspirations. With you, I've discovered a love that is not just a fleeting moment but an eternal flame that will guide us through the journey ahead. Today, I willingly and eagerly choose you as my partner, my confidante, and my love for all the days of our lives."

The words, spoken with unwavering sincerity, hung in the air like a melody. The chapel, with its ancient stones and timeless aura, seemed to resonate with the beauty of their promises. The vows, exchanged in the soft glow of candle light, were not merely words but sacred declarations of a love that was destined to endure the tests of time. As they sealed their vows with a tender exchange of rings, the chapel seemed to exhale, embracing the couple in the warm embrace of its centuries old legacy — a legacy now enriched by the vows of Jonathan and Genevieve, binding their hearts in an unbreakable union.

As the wedding ceremony reached its crescendo, a profound stillness settled over the chapel. The words spoken, laden with love and dedication, echoed in the sacred space, creating an indelible imprint on the very fabric of their shared journey. The unbreakable bond formed in those whispered promises was a testament to the enduring power of love — a love that, like the ancient stones of Graftonshire chapel, stood resilient against the tests of time.

\*\*\*

With the echoes of vows still lingering in the hallowed air of Graftonshire chapel, Jonathan and Genevieve emerged hand in hand, now united in the sacred bond of marriage. The chapel doors opened to reveal a scene bathed in the golden glow of the sun, casting a warm halo over the reception area awaiting them.

A myriad of tables adorned with delicate flowers and flickering candles greeted the couple and their guests. The gentle hum of conversations and the clinking of glasses created a symphony of joy as everyone prepared to share in the celebration of Jonathan and Genevieve's union.

The wedding breakfast, graciously hosted by both Agatha and Rosalind, awaited them under a sprawling canopy adorned with twinkling lights. The air was redolent with the aroma of delectable dishes, promising a feast not just for the palate but for the soul.

As Jonathan and Genevieve took their seats at the head table, surrounded by friends and family, a sense of warmth and camaraderie enveloped them. Agatha and Rosalind, embodying the spirit of hospitality, welcomed the guests with genuine smiles, their eyes sparkling with the joy of the occasion.

The menu, a carefully curated selection of culinary delights, reflected the rich tapestry of flavors that mirrored the couple's diverse journey. From appetizers that teased the taste buds to the main course that satisfied the heartiest of appetites, every dish held a promise of shared happiness and shared memories.

The toasts, heartfelt and sincere, resounded through the air, punctuated by the laughter and clapping of hands. As glasses were raised in honor of the newly weds, the sun painted the sky in hues of gold — a celestial backdrop to the joyous celebration. It was absolutely perfect. They could not have asked for more.

Jonathan and Genevieve, amidst the love and laughter of their cherished guests, exchanged glances that spoke volumes. The wedding breakfast became not just a feast for the senses but a feast of love — a celebration of the journey that had brought them to this moment.

Under the sprawling canopy, adorned with lights that mirrored the stars above, the celebration continued. The dance floor beckoned, and the air was filled with the rhythmic beats of music, inviting everyone to partake in the dance of joy and celebration...

As the wedding festivities unfolded beneath the sprawling canopy, joy permeated the air like a sweet melody. The celebration, now in full swing, embraced the enchanting ambiance of Graftonshire. The laughter of friends, the clinking of glasses, and the soft rustle of the breeze merged in to a symphony of celebration.

Under the gentle glow of twinkling lights, Jonathan and Genevieve found themselves at the center of the jubilation. The dance floor beckoned, a space where the rhythm of their hearts harmonized with the melodies that filled the air. As the notes of a timeless waltz began to play, the couple stepped on to the floor, surrounded by the smiling faces of their nearest and dearest. They had danced before, but it had never felt quite like this before. Now, neither of them could stop smiling because they were so pleased to have finally found where they needed to be in life. Holding onto one another was absolutely wonderful, they knew that the rest of their lives were going to be amazing. Filled with adventures. Maybe not treasure hunts, but something just as fun. They both had adventurous spirits which they knew they could explore together. They had truly found their other half, which resonated between them as they locked eyes and span around the dance floor.

As they glided across the dance floor, their movements spoke of a connection that surpassed the physical. Each step was a testament to the harmony that defined their relationship. The world around them faded into a blur, and all that remained was the embrace of the dance, the twirls and dips that mirrored the undulating cadence of their shared love.

As the final chords of the waltz echoed, Jonathan and Genevieve found themselves in the center of a circle of applauding friends and family. The dance, a prelude to a lifetime of shared moments, marked the beginning of a new chapter — a chapter where every step, every twirl, and every shared gaze held the promise of a love that would endure through the ages.

The festivities continued, the dance floor now alive with the energy of celebration, but it was time for the married couple to take a break. As the night air embraced Graftonshire Castle in its cool tendrils, Jonathan and Genevieve, now adorned in the glow of their celebration, stole a quiet moment on the balcony. The Seabrook Ruins loomed in the distance, a silent witness to the transformative journey that had brought them to this enchanted night.

The balcony, perched high above the sprawling grounds, offered a panoramic view of the castle and the surrounding landscape. The air carried the gentle hum of the festivities below, but in this secluded space, it was as if time itself slowed to savor the magic of the evening.

In Jonathan's hands, a delicately wrapped gift awaited. The anticipation in Genevieve's eyes mirrored the quiet excitement that lingered between them. With a hint of ceremony, Jonathan presented her with the elegantly adorned package, a tangible token of his sentiment.

"I have something for you, to celebrate this day."

"Oh my, you did not need to do this, Jonathan. I have not purchased anything for you."

Jonathan took Genevieve's hand and kissed her fingers. "You have given me your hand in marriage today. That is all I want. And this is not something I purchased. It is something that I have been working on for a little while now."

The outside air was filled with the soft rustling of delicate paper as Genevieve carefully unwrapped the gift Jonathan had presented to her. The anticipation hung in the air, her heart beating a little faster with each tender movement of her hands.

As the last layer of wrapping fell away, she revealed a beautifully crafted sketch in a tasteful frame. The portrait depicted her with a striking accuracy that stole her breath away. Genevieve's eyes widened in astonishment as she beheld the image before her — a true likeness captured with such precision that it seemed to breathe with life.

The details were meticulous — the way her hair cascaded in gentle waves, the subtle curve of her lips that held a hint of a smile, and the spark in her eyes that mirrored the warmth she felt inside. It was not just a drawing; it was a reflection of her essence, a piece of art that spoke to the depths of Jonathan's perception.

A gasp escaped her lips as she traced the lines with her finger tips, marveling at the intricacy of each stroke. The soft graphite shadows brought forth the nuances of her features, and the play of light and shade created a depth that seemed to capture the very essence of who she was.

Genevieve's eyes welled with emotion as she looked at the portrait, realizing the effort and thoughtfulness that Jonathan had poured into this gift. It was not just a drawing; it was a testament to the connection they shared, a visual ode to the beauty he found in her.

She turned to Jonathan, her gaze a blend of surprise and gratitude. "Jonathan, this is... extraordinary. You have captured me in a way I could not have imagined. It is as if you have seen into the depths of my soul."

A tender smile graced her lips as she continued to absorb the details of the portrait. The room seemed to fade into the background, leaving only her and the sketch, a silent exchange of emotions between the artist and his muse. In that moment, the drawing became a cherished token, a piece of art that held the magic of their connection — an intimate portrayal of her true self, seen through Jonathan's eyes. He truly did think she was beautiful, which was wonderful.

A smile graced Genevieve's lips as she looked at the sketch, the warmth of gratitude filling the quiet space between them. In the soft glow of the balcony's lights, Jonathan leaned in, and they shared a sweet, lingering kiss — a kiss that carried the echoes of their beginnings, the Seabrook Ruins standing sentinel in the background.

As they embraced on the balcony, the night sky above, the castle below, and the sketch in Genevieve's hands bore witness to a love story that had come full circle — a journey marked by fateful meetings, shared moments, and the enduring promise of a future written in the stars.

# EXTENDED EPILOGUE

*Six years later...*

It had been six long years of bliss since Genevieve and Jonathan had gotten married. Six years of joy and shared adventures that made the both of them incredibly happy. So much so that on this special day, their six year anniversary, they decided to have a lovely picnic with their family and friends too.

The laughter of children echoed against the ancient stones as Jonathan and Genevieve, now parents to twin daughters, Marie and Isabella, spread a checkered blanket under the sprawling branches of a centuries old tree. The castle, a silent guardian, stood sentinel in the background as the family gathered for a day of warmth and togetherness.

The twins, lively and full of wonder, explored the grassy expanse, their laughter like the fluttering wings of butterflies. Jonathan and Genevieve, their faces etched with the glow of parenthood, watched with pride and joy as their daughters discovered the world around them.

Lucas, a steadfast friend through the years, joined the gathering with his own family. His wife, Darla, a kindred spirit to Genevieve, shared stories and laughter, while their son, Benjamin, played alongside the twins. So much had happened in all of their lives, there was much to discuss.

The picnic basket, filled with an array of delectable treats, became a symbol of abundance and gratitude. Sandwiches, fruit, and sweet pastries adorned the spread, a feast for both the senses and the soul. As the adults engaged in animated conversation, the children's laughter provided a melodic backdrop — a symphony of familial love that resonated through the castle grounds.

The sun-dappled meadow surrounding Grafton Castle hosted not only the laughter of Jonathan, Genevieve, Lucas, and their families but also the presence of others. Harry soon joined them, now a father with his wife, Casandra, by his side, cradled their baby daughter, Ottilie in his arms. Harry and Genevieve's cousin, Eleanor, radiant as ever, arrived with her husband, Edward completing the ensemble of cherished loved ones who wished to celebrate with Jonathan and Genevieve.

As the families intermingled, sharing stories and passing bites of delicious treats, the meadow became a canvas painted with the hues of camaraderie. Harry's daughter, not yet acquainted with the world's wonders, gurgled with delight in her father's arms. Lucas's son, spirited and full of curiosity, joined the twins in their exploration of the enchanted surroundings.

As the sun dipped below the horizon, casting a warm glow over the meadow, another group approached the gathering beneath the ancient tree. Jonathan's family, cousin Agatha, and his mother Rosalind, joined the festive gathering.

The laughter of grandchildren reached a crescendo as they saw all of them together. Tiny hands grasped theirs, and hugs were exchanged amidst the backdrop of shared stories and familial love.

After eating, and when they got back home, Jonathan could not resist. He gathered the children around him to talk about his own adventures in their wonderful little town. The town which he at first thought might stifle him since he preferred to be out on the ocean, but had actually given him a much needed new lease on life. The children gathered around Jonathan, their eyes wide with anticipation as he prepared to share the tale of the journey to discover the treasure of Graftonshire. The flickering light of the fireplace cast a warm glow over their faces, creating an atmosphere of enchantment.

With a twinkle in his eye, Jonathan began to weave the story. "Once upon a time, in the heart of Graftonshire, there lay a castle steeped in history and mystery. Legends spoke of a treasure hidden within its ancient walls — a treasure that had been lost to time." As he spoke, the children leaned in, their imaginations ignited by the promise of adventure. Jonathan continued, "Now, our journey began with clues and whispers from the past. We delved into the secrets of the castle, following the footsteps of the Duke of Grafton and his long lost love. Not that we knew it at the time. We thought we were on a simple treasure hunt that took us from the Seabrook Ruins, to the Moors, and even to the River Lox."

"Oh my," Isabella whispered excitedly.

"Every step we took was a step closer to unraveling the mystery," Jonathan continued, his voice a melodic cadence. "The castle, with its creaking doors and whispering hallways, held the key to a treasure that went beyond gold and jewels. It held the essence of a love story lost to time — a love that refused to be forgotten. And that treasure hunt led us to the town's riches, and also to the ruby necklace you can see here."

As he pointed to Genevieve's neck, the children's excitement grew. As they whispered to one another, he knew that he could move on to the next part of their day. "Which is why, children, I have organized a treasure hunt for us all to embark upon. A journey through the castle grounds to uncover hidden treasures and create memories that will linger for years to come."

The announcement elicited gasps of delight from the children and smiles of anticipation from the adults. The castle, steeped in history and secrets, seemed to embrace the spirit of adventure that now filled the air.

Jonathan, armed with a weathered map, handed out copies to each participant — children and adults alike. The floor transformed into a canvas of shared excitement as the family gathered, eager to embark on the treasure hunt that Jonathan had masterfully orchestrated.

"I do hope you like what you end up finding," Jonathan called out, as the children already hurried away, ready to discover what might be found.

"What have you hidden?" Genevieve asked him excitedly, like she was about to embark on the journey herself.

"Trinkets and toys. Things the children will enjoy very much."

"I can not believe you have arranged this, Jonathan, it is truly magical."

"Well, I believe everyone deserves to have an adventure at least once in their life."

The treasure hunt unfolded like a whimsical dance through the castle grounds. Clues, carefully crafted by Jonathan, led the participants from one historical landmark to another. The castle walls seemed to whisper secrets to the treasure seekers, and the meadow became a playground for both the young and the young at heart, as Lucas and Harry joined in too.

Laughter echoed through the air as the participants unraveled each clue, the joy of discovery evident on their faces. The children, their imaginations ignited, dashed from one clue to the next, their delighted giggles merging with the rustling leaves and the soft breeze.

As the treasure hunt reached its climax, the participants found themselves at a hidden alcove beneath the castle's towering walls. Jonathan, with a mischievous glint in his eye, revealed the final treasure — a chest filled with trinkets and mementos for each participant. Something that he had individually made for all of them, and it was safe to say that they were all very happy with what they had received.

The joy of the day, now etched in the treasures collected and the memories made, radiated from the faces of the family and friends. The castle, with its ancient stones bearing witness, seemed to smile upon the scene — a scene that spoke of shared adventures, enduring love, and the timeless magic of Graftonshire.

As the laughter of family and friends echoed through the castle grounds, Jonathan and Genevieve stole away from the merriment to a quiet alcove bathed in the soft glow of twilight. The meadow, a tableau of shared joy and adventure, seemed to hush in reverence as the couple gazed upon the scene before them.

Amidst the tapestry of familial bonds, Jonathan took Genevieve's hand, their fingers entwining like vines in the evening breeze. Their eyes spoke a language known only to them — a language that whispered of shared memories, enduring love, and the promise of a future intertwined with the legacy of Graftonshire.

In the tranquil embrace of the alcove, Genevieve, her eyes sparkling with a secret delight, turned to Jonathan. With a tender smile, she revealed a delicate secret that would add another chapter to their unfolding story. "Jonathan," she whispered, her voice a soft melody, "I have something I wish to tell you, a surprise of your own." He looked at her with surprise. Jonathan thought that he was the only one who had made plans for the day. "We are going to have another adventure — a new beginning."

The words hung in the air, carrying with them the magic of anticipation. Jonathan's eyes widened with a mixture of surprise and elation, and a silent understanding passed between them. The meadow, the castle, and the surrounding woods seemed to hold their breath, as if the very elements acknowledged the profound moment unfolding in the embrace of the ancient stones.

With a gentle touch, Jonathan cupped Genevieve's face, his thumb brushing against her cheek. In that tender exchange, the unspoken promise of parenthood took root — a promise that echoed through the generations of Graftonshire's history.

In the golden glow of twilight, Jonathan and Genevieve sealed the news with a sweet kiss. The castle, a silent witness to their shared journey, stood tall in the background, its stones echoing the joyous symphony of the present and the whispers of the future.

The couple, wrapped in the warmth of the alcove, shared a moment that transcended time. The meadow, now illuminated by the soft radiance of their revelation, seemed to sigh in contentment, as if acknowledging the beauty of new beginnings beneath the watchful gaze of Grafton Castle.

**The End**

Printed by Amazon Italia Logistica S.r.l.
Torrazza Piemonte (TO), Italy